LOVE DEFINED

ELIZABETH MADDREY

OTHER BOOKS BY ELIZABETH MADDREY

Hope Ranch Series

Hope for Christmas

Peacock Hill Romance Series

A Heart Restored

A Heart Reclaimed

A Heart Realigned

Arcadia Valley Romance – Baxter Family Bakery Series

Loaves & Wishes

Muffins & Moonbeams

Cookies & Candlelight

Donuts & Daydreams

The 'Operation Romance' Series

Operation Mistletoe

Operation Valentine

Operation Fireworks

Operation Back-to-School

The 'Taste of Romance' Series

A Splash of Substance

A Pinch of Promise

A Dash of Daring

A Handful of Hope

For the most recent listing of all my books, please visit my website.

The Lord is close to the brokenhearted
and saves those who are crushed in spirit.
Psalm 34:18

1

"So, I guess that's it?" A lead weight settled in July's stomach and she leaned against the headrest of the passenger seat and closed her eyes.

Gareth's fingers closed around hers and squeezed.

"I'm not wrong though, am I?" She cracked open an eye and held his gaze.

He shook his head. "No. Probably not."

She turned and stared out the window as Gareth backed out of the parking spot and pointed the car toward home. Two more miscarriages. This time twins. Five babies she'd never know this side of heaven and none to hold. Even the ever-confident-in-his-ability Dr. DiCola couldn't honestly recommend they try IVF for a third time. "What now?"

"I think we pray about what's next. There's no need to jump into anything, Jules."

Flashes of colorful spring blossoms blurred together as they sped around the Beltway. He was probably right... though the ache in her heart screamed for action. Maybe they should go ahead and try a third time anyway. What could it hurt? July opened her mouth to ask, then snapped it shut. There were entirely too many ways trying again could hurt. Another miscarriage topped that list, followed closely by the stress on their marriage. Another miscarriage... even if they didn't pursue IVF again, getting pregnant hadn't been her problem. The thought had been that IVF would make keeping the babies easier, plus speed up the timeframe since she was working with just one fallopian tube.

But it was likely she'd end up pregnant again if they didn't decide how to keep that from happening. She didn't want to go on the pill... would Gareth ever consider a vasectomy? Though that was so permanent. Maybe she needed to look into natural family planning more closely. June had mentioned it to her last year and it might just be the perfect solution.

July blew out a breath. "Can I be honest with you?"

Gareth glanced over, brow knitting. "Always."

"I'm not... I don't know how to pray about this." She twisted her fingers in her lap. She'd spent so much time praying for a child that now... what was left to say? God had given her children. Five of them. She just didn't get to keep them long. Had she not been specific enough in her prayers? Surely God knew she'd meant that she wanted to hold her babies, nurture them... watch them grow to adulthood?

"I haven't got an easy answer. I..." He sighed and flicked on the turn signal before pulling onto their exit. "Maybe we pray about that first? Ask Him to make His will clear to us. Because I'll be honest, I thought we were doing what He wanted us to do. I don't understand why we're in this situation any more than you do."

Gareth didn't have any answers either? How did that work? He was always the one who understood when things went wrong. Her heart began to race and she swallowed the bile that tried to inch up her throat. Was this what a panic attack felt like?

"Hey." Gareth pulled into the driveway and shifted into park. "It's going to be okay. We'll figure it out."

Right. Sure they would.

With a gentle finger, Gareth lifted her chin and held her gaze. "We will. I know it doesn't seem like it's possible. And I don't have any answers, but I have faith."

She offered a short nod. "Okay. You're right."

July took a deep breath in through her nose and held it. Her heart rate slowed as she let the air escape.

"That's my girl." He leaned over and kissed her. "Come on, let's go in. You can put your feet up. Maybe we'll find something good on TV."

JULY CREPT DOWNSTAIRS to the office and prodded her computer awake. How was Gareth able to sleep? Every time she closed her eyes, babies floated through her head. The images wouldn't leave her alone while she'd flopped from one position to another, so she'd given in and gotten up. Three girls and two boys. There was no way to know for certain that those genders were right. But they felt right. And there was no point dwelling on it.

She hovered the mouse over her social media shortcut. Did she really want to see everyone's happy family photos? Or read about how terrible their jobs were? Not really. She opened her email instead. June had written—probably asking for an update. A lump lodged in her throat. That could wait 'til tomorrow. Her gaze traveled to the list of adoption resources she'd collected in a draft email. Butterflies swirled in her stomach as she began clicking the links, opening each in a new tab. There was no point in putting it off any longer. Gareth had kept up his end of the deal, now she had to keep hers.

Okay... what had June said was step one? Decide between

international or domestic, right? July blew out a breath. Where did you even start trying to figure that out? She clicked on the tab for an international adoption agency. The words swam across the screen. She blinked furiously to clear the tears that pooled in her eyes. Why wasn't "neither" an option? Because she'd promised Gareth, that's why.

She slid open the middle desk drawer and rooted around for a pen and pad of paper. She'd approach this logically. And maybe, just maybe, having lists would prove once and for all that this wasn't the right choice for them. She ripped off the top sheet and wrote "International" across the top before drawing a line down the center of the page. She labeled one side "Pros" and the other "Cons." Then she repeated the process on another sheet of paper, except the label at the top said "Domestic."

Pen in hand, she began to read.

~

"WOW. SOMEONE WAS BUSY LAST NIGHT."

July looked up from her coffee as Gareth shuffled into the kitchen, sheets of notepaper in his hand. "Couldn't sleep, figured I might as well do something useful."

He grunted, laid the papers on the counter, and grabbed the coffee carafe. "And?"

She shrugged. She'd made so many notes last night it was all just a haze. No matter what she did, the information simply swirled in her head instead of coalescing into something that resembled an opinion. And still she circled back to the fact that she didn't want to adopt. It didn't matter international or domestic. She wasn't interested.

Gareth tugged a chair out from the kitchen table and sat, lining the papers up in front of him. "So... nothing? No leanings either way?"

July frowned and set her mug down on the table so hard that coffee splashed over the lip. "I'm still processing, okay? There's a lot of information out there—too much, really—I don't know how anyone decides that this is something they want to do."

"Wait—whoa. I was just asking."

"Yeah, well. I was just answering." July shoved her chair back and stood, half-heartedly mopping at the spilled coffee with a napkin. "I'm going to take a shower."

Why couldn't he just drop it? Did they have to jump right into adoption? Couldn't they wait even a week before he had to start harping on it?

She threw her clothes into the laundry basket and stepped into the scalding water. She heaved a sigh. He'd probably only brought it up because of the notes... but what had he been doing at her computer? And even if he'd just been looking for a pen or something, once she'd answered, he should've let it drop.

She stood under the showerhead, her blood beginning to boil as the conversation replayed itself in her mind. When she'd rinsed off all the soap, she cranked the handle to shut off the water, threw a towel around herself, and slammed open the stall door.

"Gareth!"

"Yeah?" A quizzical expression on his face, he looked up from his tablet that he was reading, reclined on their bed.

She stomped across the room and jabbed a finger at him. She wasn't going to yell. Yelling wouldn't solve anything. "Just because you're in an all-fired hurry to adopt doesn't mean I am. I did some research, sure, because I'm trying to keep up my end of our deal. But that doesn't mean you get to push. Got it?"

His mouth dropped open.

July gave a curt nod and stormed back into the bathroom, shutting the door with a resounding click.

2

W hat just happened? Gareth stared at the bathroom door and shook his head. If he was supposed to chase after her, that wasn't happening right now. She couldn't get past him to get to the rest of the house. Maybe a little time in there would help her calm down and find rationality. Maybe he could even figure out what was going on.

Saturday mornings were meant for lazily reading the newspaper and technical websites while drinking entirely too much coffee. He'd gotten up shortly after July and gone into the office to get his tablet. He'd left it plugged in overnight, which meant it had been on her desk at the charging station. Her notes had been right beside his tablet and he'd taken them with him to get coffee. Mostly he'd just wanted to read them, see what she'd found out. Should he not have asked about them?

Gareth scratched his chin. It could be anything—and it was unlikely he was going to figure it out. This fell firmly in the category of July craziness. He was going to have to ask. Biting back a sigh, he swung his legs over the edge of the bed and stood. Better to do it before she had too much time for things to fester. He crossed the room and tapped on the bathroom door.

"Jules?"

"What?"

She didn't open the door. Gareth laid his hand on the knob. Had she locked it? Fine. He could talk through a door.

"Look... I'm sorry I picked up your notes. I was getting my tablet and spotted them. I really wasn't trying to push... I just, I don't know, thought you might want to talk about what you discovered."

Silence.

His shoulders sagged. What a great start to the weekend. He ran a hand through his hair. "I'm going back downstairs for more coffee. I'm sorry."

"Wait." The bathroom door clicked and squeaked open. July crossed her arms and eyed him, head askew. "Maybe I jumped the gun. I thought you were trying to get us to sign up for something right away."

How had she come up with that? He shook his head. "No."

"I... there's a lot to process. And I'm not... I don't..."

His heart broke as her eyes filled. He gathered her into his arms. "Hey. Shh. We don't have to do anything yet. You—*we*—need time to heal from the twins and everything else in that whole process."

Tears soaked the front of his t-shirt. She sniffled.

"I'm going to put your notes in the middle drawer of your desk. When you're ready, you get them out and we'll talk. But I'm not going to bring it up. Okay?"

She pulled back, her eyes searching his face. "You'd do that?"

"Of course." He kissed her forehead. "Now I'm going to get more coffee. When you're dressed, why don't we figure out what the rest of the day holds?"

July scrubbed tears off her cheeks and offered a weak smile. He winked and ambled downstairs.

He was never going to understand women.

GARETH TOOK July's hand and gave it a squeeze. The cool breeze off the Chesapeake Bay lightly ruffled his hair.

July took a deep breath and smiled as she let it out. "Annapolis was a good idea."

"It was." He glanced toward the harbor. "Want to walk down by the water or hit the shops on Main?"

She chuckled. "Do you even have to ask?"

"Shops it is. But we'll eat down on the water, right?"

"'Course." She tugged his hand. "Let's go see what we can find."

They strolled down the brick sidewalks, peering in windows and occasionally pulling open doors and browsing more thoroughly. By the time they made it all the way to Church Circle and back to the spot where they'd parked, they each carried a handful of shopping bags. Gareth's stomach rumbled.

"Let's throw these in the trunk then go find food. I'm famished."

July glanced at the clock on her phone. "No wonder. It's nearly two. Too bad it's not crab season yet... where do you want to eat?"

Gareth frowned. She was right, it was still too early for crabs. "I had my heart set on crabs—totally forgot we're a few weeks ahead of our usual Annapolis start-of-crab-season trip. So... I guess I don't really care. Anywhere you've been dying to try out?"

"Let's try over there." She pointed to a federal blue building off to their left. "I've heard it's good and you can always get crab cakes. It's not quite the same, I know, but it's better than nothing."

July slipped her arm through his as they crossed the street and ducked into the historic-looking tavern. He smiled. How long had it been since they'd had such a relaxing time together? Ever since things fell apart in the fall, they'd been working to put their relationship first. But with the initial IVF pregnancy, subsequent miscarriage, more treatment, and then another pregnancy... things had slipped back into hectic mayhem. Even their dinners out on the weekend turned to discussions of babies. Today was the first day in a long time that had been just about the two of them.

"We should come out here more often. It's not that far, and it's nice to be away from home and near the water."

July smiled at him over the top of her menu. "I was just thinking something similar. It's been a nice day, hasn't it?"

He nodded and snapped his menu shut. He was getting the crab cakes. It might be predictable, but his taste buds yearned for that sweet crustacean. If he had to eat it breaded and fried today, that was okay by him. "Want to see about renting a sailboat after lunch, spend some time on the Bay before we head home?"

"You know what? I do. I really do."

3

June bounced her knee and glanced around the sanctuary. Where were July and Gareth? She'd been leaving messages for her sister since Friday afternoon. With no response. It probably meant July had had another miscarriage, but June wasn't going to give up hope until she heard it directly from her sister.

Toby laid his hand on her knee. "You're shaking the whole pew."

"Sorry. I'm just anxious... and running out of excuses for the lack of a call from July."

He sighed. "What happened to 'no news is good news'?"

June shook her head. "I just have a feeling. And it's not like July to keep good news to herself."

Toby arched a brow. "Really? 'Cause that wasn't always the case."

"Okay. Fine. You're right. And even if we're sisters, I'm not entitled to anything, I know that. But I just thought this time it was for sure going to be all right. Wouldn't she be shouting it from the rooftops?"

"Probably. But just try to remember that it's not our business. Not really. And if she doesn't want to talk about it, you need to respect that."

June nodded. He was right. It had been a hard lesson to learn over the past eighteen months as she and her sister had navigated the troubled waters of family building. It was still a challenge. They'd always shared everything... why did that have to change now?

A flash of red hair caught her eye and June turned. July and Gareth slid into a pew at the back. June gave a small wave as the organ launched into the prelude. Well, at least they were here. She'd catch them after the service. Or maybe they'd be in small group.

June struggled to keep her attention on the sermon. Would she have called July, if their situations were reversed? Of course she would. So what was the problem? Was July worried about what June would say? Maybe there was a reason for that...though she'd gotten better about not mentioning adoption lately. A lot of that was because there was nothing to say, but there had still been several times she could have said something and she hadn't. That had to count for something.

She drew circles down the edge of her sermon notes. Why wasn't there any news on the adoption front? Faith, their social worker, said not to worry, but it had been almost six months. Shouldn't their profile have been shown to someone at least once? Was there something wrong with them, or their portfolio, that no one even looked like a potential match?

Toby nudged her as the congregation stood for the benediction. "You okay?"

June shrugged. "I guess. Let's go see if July and Gareth are going to small group."

They wove through the exiting crowd. Her sister waited at the back of the sanctuary.

"Hey. Sorry I didn't call back." Dark circles sank into the

skin beneath July's eyes. "I couldn't bring myself to say it out loud."

June's stomach plummeted and she pulled her sister into a hug. "I'm sorry. So sorry."

July eased back. "Thanks. I think Gareth's waiting at the car —we were going to try and make it to small group but... I think we're both too beat."

"Do you want me to mention anything? Or..." June tried to put herself in her sister's place. Would it be easier to have people know without having to be the one to tell them? Or did that make it worse?

"Would you?"

"Of course."

July let out a long breath. "That'd be great. Then maybe next week...could you also tell them we're not ready to talk about it, maybe encourage them to follow our lead and not bring it up?"

"Will do. You don't want meals or anything, right? You know Laura's going to ask, so I want to know what to say."

"Good thinking. No. We're good. But... we still on for lunch tomorrow?"

June grinned. "You bet. I'll see you then."

~

"THAT WENT WELL, I THINK." Toby settled into the couch with a groan and propped his feet on the coffee table. "It seems like everyone understood July and Gareth not wanting a whole lot of overt sympathy right now."

June nodded and perched on the cushion next to him. "It's a good class. I'm glad we went back, even though all the baby talk was hard for a while."

"Yeah. Thankfully that's tapered off some." Toby cocked his head to the side. "What's going on with you, June?"

She laughed. He knew her too well. "Why do you think we haven't had at least one potential match yet? Is there something wrong with our portfolio?"

Toby frowned. "It's only been six months, babe. They said the average was eighteen. And that's the average—we could end up on the high end."

"Or the low end. I was really hoping we'd be on the lower side. After everything we've been through..." June ran a hand through her hair.

"It takes time. I know it's hard to be patient, but that's all we can do. Have you heard from Faith lately?" Toby squeezed her knee.

"I emailed her the other day. Nothing new. She said basically the same thing you did: it takes time and we just have to be patient and pray. I'm not very good at that."

His lips curved into a smile. "I'm not either."

"Ha. When was the last time you worried about it—or anything?"

"Just because I maintain my outward calm doesn't mean I don't worry. I'm just trying to remember that God's got this."

"What if the answer to this is 'no,' too?"

"Then we'll figure out how to deal with that. Right now, we can just step out in faith and ask God to direct our steps."

He wasn't wrong. But it was annoying. Would it be so terrible if God gave them some kind of concrete sign that they were doing the right thing?

"What are you watching?" June glanced over as Toby clicked on the TV.

"Not sure. Thought I'd just flip channels and see what I could find. Do you have a preference?"

"Nah. I'm going to go check my email, maybe do some reading on this new programming language they're talking about using on the next phase of our project." June kissed

Toby's cheek and stood. "I'll come check on you in a bit, see if you found something worthwhile."

Toby's chuckle followed her out of the room and into the office. She logged into her work email first. Why did she get messages on the weekend? Some people needed to learn about rest and recuperation. At least the questions were relatively easy to answer. Nothing from her team, which was good. There wasn't enough in the budget for weekend work, and they were doing all right on their deadline right now anyway. No point in anyone going crazy until it was necessary.

June switched to her personal email account. She should really get off some of the infertility message groups she'd joined last year. At this point, there wasn't any new information to learn and, well, it was depressing. She selected all the messages from the groups and deleted them, unread.

Mom had written. She bit back a groan and clicked it open, skimming for anything important. Nothing jumped out, so she went back to the inbox. She'd read it more thoroughly later. Who was this last email from? June drummed her fingers on the keyboard before clicking. Her heart raced as she devoured the words. Faith was out sick but a new birth mother had come in yesterday and they thought she and Toby might be a good match. Did they want to be included? She did a little victory dance in her seat. Of course they wanted to be included! She sent up a quick prayer of thanks for the sign, just when she needed it, and ran out to the living room to tell Toby.

4
————————

"You look like you're about ready to burst. What's going on?" July scooted over on the bench to give her sister more room.

June plopped down, a grin spreading over her face. "We got an email last night—they're including us in a batch of profiles that a birthmother is going to look at today."

Well that figured. Of course June was going to get good news when she was dealing with bad news. She forced a smile. "That's great."

"It's not a guarantee or anything." June's smile faded. "And I should have just kept quiet. I'm sorry. I know you're still hurting."

July shrugged. "Doesn't matter, that's good news and you need to be able to share it. When will you know?"

"I'm not sure. I guess it just depends on how long it takes for the young woman to make a decision."

"Do you have any details?"

June shook her head. "Not many. They said the girl is seventeen and the baby is with her long-term boyfriend. They're both healthy and she's been getting prenatal care. Right now, that's all we have to go on. So I'm focusing on praying that she finds the right family... and hoping that it's us."

"Uh-huh." July shook her head. "This is me, June. You've already started thinking up names and decorating your nursery, haven't you?"

Pink stole across June's cheeks. "The nursery is kind of already done anyway. Toby's mom got us so much stuff when we were there at Thanksgiving... but okay, fine. Maybe I'm pinning my hopes on this. Is that wrong?"

"I don't know. Probably not. But what happens if she chooses someone else?"

"Then I guess we deal with the disappointment. How is this any different than being excited about a positive pregnancy test?"

July sighed. It probably wasn't different. But what June didn't seem to realize is that after a few miscarriages, it's harder to get excited about the positive tests, because they're just a portent of potential heartbreak ahead. At least that's how it was for her. Maybe other women were able to keep being positive and thinking that this one was going to be the one that stuck... but it had never worked for her. "I don't want to see you hurt is all. And the statistics are rough."

"Maybe so. But could you try to be at least a little happy for me? I get that this is a hard time for you, and I realize I should've probably kept it to myself... but I was hoping you'd pray about it with us." June opened her lunch bag and frowned at the contents. "Why am I always surprised when I see what I have for lunch? I'm the one who packed it."

July laughed. "I have that problem, too." She paused and reached over to squeeze her sister's hand. "And of course I'll pray."

$\sim$

JULY TUCKED her lunch bag and purse in her desk and dropped her head against the back of her chair. She was happy for her sister. She was. But she couldn't stop the sinking sensation, either. If June and Toby adopted, wouldn't that just give Gareth more ammo for pushing them to do the same? And, okay, sure. The outcome was exactly what they wanted, but... why couldn't she get excited about it? Wasn't it possible that adoption wasn't right for everyone? Even if they wanted children but couldn't conceive?

Her desk phone rang. July checked the clock and groaned. She normally enjoyed working with the small business clients on her schedule, but this particular organic farmer was a colossal pain. Mr. Gorman was a delight, but his wife... she'd taken a few community college accounting classes and wanted to second guess everything. July had come close several times to suggesting they take over their own work if Mrs. Gorman was convinced she could do better. She never quite got the words out. Not only would it be bad for July professionally, she couldn't in good conscience allow Mr. Gorman to put his livelihood in danger that way. But it didn't mean she couldn't try to trade the account at every possible opportunity. Unfortunately, no one else in the firm was biting.

The phone rang and she cradled the handset against her shoulder as she pulled up the Gorman Farms account on her computer. "This is July."

"Hello, dear. Do you have a minute?"

Oh great. On the positive side, it wasn't the Gormans. But... "Hi, Mom. What's up?"

"Your father and I were just talking about how much we missed you two, and he made a passing comment that, well, it struck me as worth exploring. So I figured better to call now, before we talked ourselves out of it."

"Oh?"

"Do you have any Easter plans yet?"

Easter plans? Who made Easter plans? "Well, just church. Pastor Brown has a really nice sunrise service on Easter Sunday. It's a great culmination to the week of services focusing on the Crucifixion. It's his favorite part of the church calendar, and it shows. Why?"

"We thought we might come down. You and June have both mentioned how great the services are, and frankly I could do with an infusion of that. Besides, we haven't seen June since Thanksgiving and it's been much longer for you."

Was she going to mention the exact day count? There was no question that her mom knew it, probably to the minute. "I know. It's been a rough couple of months, Mom. I'm sorry we haven't been out to see you."

"Oh, July. That's not what I meant and you know it." Her mother gave an exasperated sigh. "Can we come out or is that going to be inconvenient for you?"

July winced. Having Mom visit was never high on her list, but it had been a while. "Of course. We'd love to have you."

"Wonderful. I'll have your father figure out the arrangements and send them to you. He's talking about driving, but he has so many points on his airline card I'm going to see if I can't talk him into flying. It's so much more convenient."

July stifled a groan. It might be more convenient for them, but it made life more difficult for everyone else since they refused to rent a car. But there was no point in trying to have that conversation, particularly not when she was at work. "Okay. Great. I have to run, Mom, my other line's ringing."

"Love you, dear."

"You too." July pushed the button for her second line. "This is July."

"Hi, July, it's the Gormans for our conference call. Sorry to be late calling in."

July took a bottle of aspirin from her desk drawer and shook two into her hand, swallowing them dry. "Not a problem at all. I've got your file open already. Let's start with January, shall we?"

"Did you know 'Easter plans' are a thing now, apparently?" July wriggled over to make room on the couch for Gareth and leaned over to steal a chip from the bowl he settled in his lap.

"Hey." He swatted her hand. "I asked if you wanted some, you said no. And no, what are 'Easter plans'?"

She snitched another chip, grinning at his frown. "I didn't want my own bowl. In our case, 'Easter plans' means that my parents are coming to visit, because we didn't have anything else scheduled that I could think of when she called me after lunch."

Gareth shook his head. "Well, it has been a while since we saw them."

"She mentioned that. At least I didn't get a litany of the months, days, and hours since our last visit."

He chuckled. "Lucky you. When will they come?"

July shrugged. "She said Dad would email the details when they had them hashed out. He wants to drive, she wants to fly. You're not upset?"

"Nah. I like your parents, when they're not making you crazy."

Usually he'd be annoyed that she'd agreed without talking to him first. "That was easy."

"Sorry. Was I supposed to be irritated? I can probably manage it, if it'll help? I just don't really see the point."

"Yeah, that's okay. I imagine June'll grouse enough for everyone. After all, they went up for Thanksgiving. And—I almost forgot—they've potentially got a placement. I wonder if they'll know one way or the other by Easter?"

Gareth's eyebrows shot up. "When'd you hear about this?"

"Lunch. I was going to call you and mention it after my conference call with the Gormans, but Mom called and then things got busy."

"That's exciting—so quick."

July frowned. Was it fast? It'd been several months—she couldn't say exactly how many. She had to stop tuning out when June brought up adoption. It was going to get her in trouble. Soon. As for exciting... dinner twisted sourly in her stomach. "I still... it's not..."

Gareth squeezed her knee. "I'm happy for them. I'm not trying to push you. We can get there in our own time. In some ways, it's good to have them blazing the trail."

Bile swam up her throat. She wet her lips. How was she ever going to convince him that it wasn't the right decision for them?

5

June flopped back onto the bed. What a day. Every time the phone rang, her heart had accelerated, wondering if it would be the agency. The only thing to come of it, though, was the feeling that she'd had entirely too much coffee. She was wired and drained at the same time. Why hadn't they called?

"Napping?" Toby kicked his shoes toward the closet and stretched out next to her.

"Nope. Just trying to get my muscles to quit buzzing. I was so worked up about our profile being shown today that I basically ran on adrenaline."

A corner of his mouth quirked up. "I struggled with that myself. Given that you didn't call me, I'm guessing we haven't heard anything yet?"

She shook her head and rolled to her side to face him. "And now I've got worst case scenarios running through my head."

"Don't jump to conclusions. Maybe they just got busy. Or maybe they like to wait a day just to be sure that the birthparents are sure about their choice. I can't imagine anything worse than getting told you were chosen one day and then getting slammed the next day if the birthparents changed their minds."

Her stomach clenched. "Is that even a possibility?"

"Of course it is." Toby frowned. "You remember the intro seminar and our training class don't you? She's got ten days after the baby's born. So while, yeah, it'll be great if we're chosen, that doesn't guarantee anything."

June swallowed. Okay, sure, those words had been spoken, but they hadn't seemed real. Now, when they were staring down the actual possibility of being chosen, the reality began to solidify. Ten days after the baby is born. Maybe they should take their agency up on the offer of temporary foster care just in case—no. No, they'd risk it. Ten days of bonding and having that baby with them. She wasn't going to miss out on that. And if the unthinkable happened...

The phone rang. June's breath caught in her throat. Wide-eyed, she stared at Toby and pointed to the phone on his nightstand with a shaking hand.

Toby sat up and grabbed the handset. He cleared his throat. "Hello?"

June scooted up and angled her head. He tilted the handset, but she couldn't quite make out the words. She mouthed the words, "Put it on speaker."

He squinted at the phone before pressing a button.

Faith's voice filled the bedroom. "...wanted a couple with dogs, since both of them grew up with Labradors. Don't let it discourage you, though. There really is a match for everyone out there, it's just a matter of finding them, okay?"

June slumped backward, her head cracking on the headboard.

Toby winced and shook his head. "Okay. Sure. Thanks for calling to let us know."

She watched him set the phone gently back in its cradle and

rub his neck. He looked so calm. Tears filled her eyes before brimming over and streaming down her cheeks.

"Hey." Toby pulled her into his arms and began rubbing small circles on her back. "This was the first time we've been included in the portfolios shown. We knew it wasn't likely that we'd be chosen that quickly."

June buried her head in his shoulder. He may have known that, but she hadn't. If anything, she'd known it *was* going to be fast now that they were done chasing their tails with treatment. Shouldn't something finally be easy for them? Didn't God owe them that much at least? Her breath hitched. Okay, fine. Maybe God didn't owe them anything... she'd put those thoughts to rest. Mostly. But still... couldn't something finally go their way?

JUNE LEANED back in her chair and pressed her fingers against her right eye. She'd woken up with a slight headache, but the dull throb had turned into an unrelenting pounding after staring at her monitor for an hour. None of the members of her team were on track to meet their deadline, but no one could explain what the problem was. Evidently they were struggling to understand what they needed to do, but so far none of the meetings she'd held were helping. Was she going to have to sit with each of them and hold their hands? Why couldn't anything in her life happen on a reasonable schedule?

She sighed. It hadn't been that long. Not really. But even though Toby was right, it didn't make the sense of loss any less. Weren't they on the right path this time? Wasn't *this* what God had been waiting for them to do? Now He could finally bless them... right? Or were they on the wrong track again? Was she just too impatient? Okay, that was a stupid question. Patience. She'd work on patience.

"Knock, knock." Bob poked his head in her office door. "Got a minute?"

"Sure." She wasn't making headway on her work, so why not?

Bob lowered himself into one of her guest chairs, the pounds he'd recently been packing on oozing over the arms. "Where are we on next week's deadline?"

June shook her head. "About the same place we were last week when you asked. I don't know what's going on—no one's talking to me."

Bob frowned. "Do I need to ask for an extension?"

She chewed on her lower lip. It was absolutely what they needed, but it came with penalties on all sides. The customer had fees for missing deadlines, and it opened up the possibility of exercising the cancellation clause in the contract, which would lead to even bigger consequences in the office. You didn't just blow off a three-million dollar contract. Aside from that, it wouldn't look good on her performance report. She was still in the early stages of her team lead role... if she demonstrated an inability to get the work done... better not to go there. Just the thought of job hunting left a solid mass of lead in her stomach. On the other hand, if she said no and then they missed the deadline without having asked for an extension it would look even worse. She closed her eyes. "I don't know, Bob. I want to say no, but...I just don't know."

"It's a tough call. Tell you what, talk to your team, explain it to them clearly, and then get back to me. I can put off asking for another day, maybe two. But after that, we're going to look bad if we don't give them advance notice and still miss the deadline." He heaved himself to his feet. "The small conference room is open right now, if you want to use it."

When Bob had disappeared down the hall, June lowered her head to the desk. Just what she needed, a meeting with her useless team. Except that they hadn't always been useless.

Maybe she could figure out what was going on this time. Though why would it be any different today than it had been for the last month? With a deep breath and firm mental shake, she stood, gathered a notepad and pen, and headed into the hall.

When everyone had gathered in the conference room and the grumbling quieted, or at least dimmed, June clasped her hands together over her notepad. "From the status reports last week, I know we're not making much headway. I need to find out where we are and how it's looking in terms of finishing this deliverable on time. If we're going to ask for an extension, we have to do it soon—tomorrow at the latest—or we end up with egg on our face no matter what. So we're going around the table and everyone is going to say what they're working on and when they can expect to have it finished. If you're stuck, explain the problem and we'll brainstorm a solution. Jill, let's start with you."

Jill crossed her arms. "I'm doing the best I can, but I'm waiting on Henry to get his piece finished so we can integrate them."

"Look, my daughter's been sick and my wife can't take any more time off. I'll get it done—I just need another day, maybe two." Henry frowned across the table at Jill.

Great. Bickering between team members was just what she needed. Her eyelid twitched as a throb began to build behind her eye. She blew out a breath. "Okay, that handles Jill and Henry. Phong?"

He shrugged. "My piece is finished. I've been waiting on Henry as well."

"Have you offered to help? If Henry's been out..." Did she have to do everything for these people?

"I don't need help. I just need a day or two, and if you had kids, you'd understand instead of pushing me to meet some arbitrary deadline." Henry pushed away from the table. "If you're in such a hurry and I'm holding everyone up, this meeting is a waste of my time."

The blood drained from her face and a heavy weight settled on June's shoulders as Henry stalked out of the room. "Anyone have a problem they need help with? Jill, do you think you're set, once Henry's piece is done?"

"I won't know for sure until then, but yeah, I think so." Jill shrugged.

"Okay. Phong, go see how you can help Henry. There's got to be something he can off-load to you. If he won't, come and get me. We don't have a day or two. I need to know if we should go ahead and take the hit by asking for an extension or if we think we can squeeze things in under the wire. If Henry's daughter is ill, I don't think we should count on him having consistent hours for the next week, so be ready to pick up slack if that's what we need to do."

After Jill and Phong left, June closed her eyes. Her head dropped back against the chair. How dare Henry blame her. Just because she didn't have kids didn't mean she didn't understand. Maybe she didn't *know* fully, but she could put herself in his shoes and imagine. Besides which, he should've said something sooner. Sick or not, kids weren't an excuse for letting down your team.

6

G areth checked over his shoulder before pulling out July's desk drawer. He took out the list of adoption pros and cons and skimmed them. There were more cons than pros. Did she realize that? He frowned. Maybe he could add in a few of the pros that were missing... but would she notice? Of course she would. For one thing, his hand-writing was terrible. Too bad she hadn't typed the list. Why were some of the obvious pros missing though? Like the end result being a family?

He dropped into his chair and stared at the papers, his stomach coiling in on itself like a snake getting ready to strike. She didn't want to adopt. She'd said as much before, but this made it clear just how serious she was about that. So... what did that mean in the long run? He could try to change her mind. Gareth sorted through various arguments that might appeal to her logical side and discarded them. At the end of the day, a logical argument wasn't going to suffice. Even he could counter every one of his points, and he was on board with adoption. Would an emotional appeal work?

Gareth tipped his head back to frown at the ceiling. His

heart still bled from each of July's miscarriages. But so did hers. What would a failed placement do to them? It was practically guaranteed that there'd be at least one false start before a successful adoption, wasn't it? His heart sank. How, after all the heartache they'd already been through, did you deal with that?

Okay, so maybe she was right to be opposed. What did that mean for them? They weren't going to be able to conceive naturally and, given the results of their treatments and the doctor's recommendation against pursuing further treatment, it was unlikely that they'd be able to carry to term even if they found someone willing to work with them on another IVF. Childless. It meant they would end up childless. That sounded so final. So... lonely.

He sighed and closed his eyes. He'd never pictured a life without kids. Even as an older teenager, a family—with multiple children—had always been in his mental image. As soon as he'd met July, she'd been the woman running around with him chasing those kids. Now... now he'd have to reimagine the whole of the future that stretched out in front of them. But could he?

"We have nicer chairs for napping in you know."

His eyes flew open. July nudged his chair, sending it careening into the desk.

"I wasn't napping. I was thinking. When did you get home?"

"Just now. Thinking about wh..." Her eyes drifted to the papers on his leg. "Oh."

Heat crept up his neck. He'd wanted to get them put away before she got home. Knowing July, just looking at the lists could be considered pushing. "I wasn't—I was just... you really don't want to adopt, do you?"

July's gazed fixed on him for several heartbeats before her head slowly shook from side to side. She sank into her chair and scooted until their knees touched, her voice a whisper. "I'm sorry."

"Don't be sorry." Gareth covered her hands with his. "These lists aren't inaccurate. I think you might have missed some of the possible positives, but I get it. I just figured we'd take it a day at a time and see where that left us—only worry about them if we had to."

Her shoulders slumped and a hint of defensiveness crept into her tone. "You know I'm not good at that. And with kids... I just don't see taking on responsibility for someone else's life if you haven't thought through all the possibilities."

Had she done that with each of the pregnancies? Probably. It was just how she was. He nodded and stacked the papers together, tapping them on his leg as he blew out a breath. "Okay. We'll table the idea. I'm not ready to say we'll dismiss it completely, but for now—for the foreseeable future—we'll put it aside."

Disbelief flitted across her face before her lips split into a grateful smile. "You'd do that?"

"Of course I will. I love you, Jules."

She crawled into his lap and wound her arms around him, burying her face in his neck. "I love you, too."

GARETH WATCHED the shadows flicker across the bedroom wall. July's deep, even breathing next to him failed to have its usual soporific effect. Giving up on children was the right thing to do. If he'd had any doubts, the lack of tension between him and July this evening would've made it apparent. It had been eating at her, whether she realized it or not. Was that his fault? He'd made her promise that they'd consider adoption when he agreed to try treatment, true. But had she really thought he'd hold her to it when push came to shove? If she'd just explained... no... she'd tried. He could see it now, looking back. He just hadn't heard.

He flopped onto his back and pillowed his head on his arm. Were there other things he wasn't seeing? Other areas where he should be more attuned to July but was so blinded by his own agenda that he was missing the stress he was putting on their relationship?

"You okay?" Sleep slurred her words as she struggled to sit up.

"Yeah, sorry. Can't sleep. I'll go downstairs."

Scrubbing a hand over her face, July yawned, her jaw cracking. "Stay. What's bothering you?"

"Am I a good husband?"

She frowned, her eyebrows drawing together. "Of course. Why would you even ask that?"

He scoffed. "Why wouldn't I? Look back over the last eighteen months... I haven't exactly been the poster boy for Prince Charming."

"Yes you have. It's just that we ran into the reality that Happily Ever After is only for fairy tales. I don't imagine that Charming—or any of the other princes you can think up—would have done any better. This is uncharted territory, Gar. We did okay. Sure, it was bumpy...but you have to do some off-roading to reach all the best destinations."

"We're okay?"

July slid closer and snuggled against him. She trailed her fingers down his arm and across his chest. "We're even better than okay."

7

July checked that her Bluetooth microphone was connected, and then dialed June. This conversation couldn't wait for lunch—if her sister could even get away for lunch today. It was as if she'd lost fifty pounds. The birds sang sweeter, the sky glowed a softer blue. And she hadn't had to be the bad guy. Gareth had figured it out on his own—and been okay with it. That was the real miracle.

"Hey, Jules. Shouldn't you be at work?"

"Yeah, I'm a little late getting started today. Gareth and I had a long talk last night."

"Uh oh."

"No. That's the thing, it wasn't bad at all. I was worried it was going to be when I walked in and saw him with my pro and con lists for adoption, but he finally got it. He said we don't have to adopt if I don't want to—that he understands my reservations." Silence stretched over the line. July furrowed her brow and glanced down at her phone. It said the call was still connected. "June? You there?"

"Yeah, yeah, I'm here. That's great."

"Think you could be any less enthusiastic?" Fine, her sister was all gung-ho about adopting, but couldn't June at least understand—or try to understand—where she was coming from?

June's sigh crackled in her ear. "I'm glad you and Gareth are on the same page. I truly am. But I wish you didn't have to be so negative about adopting. If everything goes like I hope it will, you're going to be an aunt to a baby who was adopted. Are you going to be able to handle that? Will you love your niece or nephew, or are you just going to see them as a bundle of negative possibilities?"

Where had that come from? "What? Of course I'll love them. What does that have to do with anything?"

"It has everything to do with everything! You're so down on adopting, making it sound like it's some kind of last choice, barrel-scraping effort for losers, what am I supposed to think?"

July kneaded her suddenly aching temples. Had she done that? Nothing immediately came to mind... but she didn't always remember her conversations word for word. And what she said wasn't always what June heard. Or what she meant. "I'm sorry. That was never my intention... I..."

"Don't. Okay? Right now it's not any kind of immediate concern anyway. Who knows, we may never get chosen. Maybe you'll be lucky and not have to worry about it. Look, I have to go. I'll catch you later, okay?"

July's phone switched back to the main screen as the call ended. That could've gone better.

HER CALL with June had set a precedent for the day. By noon, July was ready to pack up and head home. She'd fielded two disastrous calls from Mrs. Gorman before finally involving her boss. At least now he understood why no one wanted these people as their client. He'd smoothed over this issue, but it was just a matter of time before the woman came up with some other brainstorm that, left unchecked, was guaranteed to end up with someone in prison. Or at least paying some hefty fines. Why couldn't people just let the experts do their job? That was what they got paid for.

July had also left three voicemails for June, with no response. It was possible that her sister was just busy at work... but it felt like June was ducking her calls. Maybe she hadn't been as supportive as she could've been with the whole adoption thing but June was blowing it out of proportion too, wasn't she?

A groan slipped out when her desk phone rang. Now what?

"This is July."

"Hi, July, it's Dad."

"Hey, Dad. What's up?"

"I was calling to give you our details for Easter. Got a pen handy?"

Easter. She'd forgotten about Easter. And she hadn't mentioned it to June yet. Great. She forced a smile. "Of course, hit me."

Her dad rattled off an itinerary that took them through Indiana, Kentucky, Tennessee, Georgia, North and South Carolina, and finally got them to the DC area for Easter.

"Does Mom know you're planning this?"

"Oh, she'll be fine once she realizes she gets to see so many different places we've always talked about visiting. Plus, she loves to drive."

"You sure? She really sounded like she wanted to fly when you first talked about coming out..."

"Pfft. Trust me. I know your mother. Anyway, if you think of anything you want from somewhere along the way, just let me know and we'll pick it up for you. We'll head home the more typical route—though I'm eyeing a slight detour up to Niagara Falls. We haven't been there since our honeymoon."

July made a non-committal sound. If Mom wanted to fly and Dad was planning a huge road trip like this... well, it was good she didn't live at home anymore. She didn't need to witness those fireworks. Dad sounded so excited, it was likely he'd win that argument and they'd drive. But who knew what passive aggressive punishment her mother would be meting out the whole time they were in town.

When she hung up with her dad, July dialed her sister. Leaving this news on voicemail wasn't a bad thing.

"This is June."

Of course she picked up this time. "It's July."

Her sister sighed. "I got your voicemails. It's fine, okay?"

"Thanks. Not actually why I was calling this time though. I just got off the phone with Dad. He and Mom are coming out for Easter—and they're making it a road trip." July recited the highlights of the multi-state tour their dad had outlined.

"Mom's okay with that? That's... a lot of driving."

July snickered. "Those are almost exactly the same words I used. Dad said she was going to love it."

June groaned. "She's going to be grousing the whole time she's here, isn't she?"

"Very likely."

"Oh, goody."

"Yeah, something like that. Anyway, just figured I'd give you a heads up. They can stay with us."

"No... you had them last time, it's only fair that we take our turn." June breathed a heavy sigh. "When did they say they'd be here?"

"Dad's talking about getting in that Friday, late, and leaving on Tuesday or Wednesday."

"I'll let Toby know. Thanks."

July hung up and dug a granola bar out of her desk drawer. Her mother was going to give birth to an entire herd of cattle.

Possibly also some sheep. You'd think, after so many years of marriage, her dad would have a clue.

～

"How was your day?" July dropped her purse on its hook and kicked off her shoes.

Gareth shrugged. "Okay, I guess. Nothing to write home about. You?"

"I've had better. Mrs. Gorman is going to be the death of me. Or, at least of my sanity. That woman should just go get a degree in accounting, take her CPA exam, and be done with it. Of course, then she wouldn't be able to come up with wacky ideas to increase their business write-offs, because she'd know they were illegal." July rubbed the back of her neck. "And I got my dad's itinerary for their Easter visit. I'm expecting Mom to call and explode as soon as she hears about it."

"Do I want to know?" Gareth propped his feet on the coffee table.

"He wants to drive. And see the majority of the Midwest in the process. Plus a jaunt to Niagara on their way home."

Gareth's eyebrows shot up. "That's... a big road trip. I thought your mother hated to drive."

"She does. Everyone knows this. Except, apparently, Dad, who's convinced she's going to love it."

"Wow. I'd pay good money to be a fly on the wall when that goes down."

July grinned. "'Til you got swatted to make a point."

"There's that. What's for dinner?"

July cocked her head to the side. It was his turn to cook, as far as their loose definition of turns went. But he looked... off. Maybe he was just tired, or something was going on at work that he couldn't talk about yet? "I'll go see what we've got."

She ambled into the kitchen and stared into the fridge. She

took a surreptitious look over her shoulder. He was just sitting there. He hadn't turned on the TV, he didn't have a book... it wasn't like him. Should she push? July pulled out the ingredients for chicken curry. Maybe something spicy would cheer him up. And if it didn't... then she'd push.

8

"July just goes on and on about how awesome it is that Gareth isn't going to 'force' her to adopt, like I'm supposed to be excited about that. She doesn't see how her attitude could possibly hurt me. After all, why should I care that my kids' aunt is going to consider them second-class citizens in the family?" June dropped her hands into her lap and laced her fingers together. "And she never even asked about the potential placement. Not like I had good news to share... but it would've been nice to be asked, maybe get some sympathy."

Lydia reached across the coffee shop table and squeezed June's hand. "Sorry. They chose someone else?"

June nodded as tears burned behind her eyes. She swallowed, refusing to cry.

"Do you think if she'd known you weren't chosen she might have approached it differently?" Lydia picked at the corner of the coffee cup sleeve.

Would she? July didn't usually set out to be obnoxious—she managed to stumble into it quite well without effort. "Yeah...

probably. I just... I don't understand why she's so adamantly against adoption."

"Is it adoption in general, or just for her and Gareth?"

"It's the same thing."

Lydia frowned. "Is it?"

"Of course it is. You're either in favor of something or not. That's just how things work." June scowled into her coffee.

"I'm typically all about the absolutes. I flirted enough with all the justifications on the grey scale to know that they're just that—justifications. But I don't think this one is that easy."

"What do you mean?"

Lydia shifted in her seat and crossed one leg over the other, bouncing it up and down. "Adoption seems to me to be one of the few things you can be entirely in support of from an abstract sense, but not willing to undertake for your own family-building without being inconsistent."

June shook her head.

"Hear me out." Lydia sipped her coffee. "The majority of people who say they're pro-life are going to, in an abstract way, think adoption is a wonderful thing. In situations where it doesn't make sense for someone to get married and parent— or to decide to be a single parent—and there isn't a family member willing to raise the child for you, adoption is always going to be seen as the next best option. So people will generally say they're pro-adoption, because really, what's not to support? The baby gets to live and thrive in a loving home. But when the rubber meets the road—either as one in the situation of placing a baby for adoption or a couple adding to their family through adoption—it can be trickier for some people."

"So what are you saying?" June crossed her arms. "I should be thrilled for my sister that she isn't going to adopt?"

Lydia shrugged. "If that's the decision that she and Gareth came to mutually, then yes. Or, at least try to understand that their choice doesn't say anything about your own. And failing all of that, show her some grace."

June clamped her teeth down on a sharp retort. Grace. When was someone going to show *her* some grace? Didn't July ever have to step up to the grace plate and dish it out? Okay, maybe that wasn't completely fair... she'd worry about that later. "I guess. Enough. What's new with you?"

Lydia pulled her lower lip between her teeth and set down her coffee. "You can't tell anyone, okay?"

June nodded.

Lydia leaned across the table and lowered her voice. "I hit nine weeks yesterday. I've been to the doctor and heard the heartbeat. He said everything looks good... we're cautiously optimistic, but still not telling anyone until after the first trimester's over."

June's lips spread into a grin. "Oh, congratulations. That's incredibly good news. Kevin's got to be over the moon."

"He is. Though he's also worried—the miscarriage last year and then not conceiving since—it's shaken him. I'm not sure he'll fully appreciate that this is happening until the baby's in his arms."

July could probably understand that better than June, but it made sense. After this experience with a placement, June was going to work to keep her hope in check until they knew one way or the other. Easier said than done. She was still jumping every time the phone rang, hoping it was another opportunity to be added to the stack for someone to consider. "That's hard. Does it bother you?"

"Nah. I think, if the situation was reversed, I'd be the same way. But between the morning sickness and water retention, there's no avoiding that this pregnancy is real. I just pray, constantly it feels like, that God will let it go full term." Lydia looked down at her hands. "I don't think I could take another miscarriage. And Kevin? It would destroy him."

"Can I tell Toby?" If she said no, it was going to be a hard promise to keep.

"'Course. Just... can you not mention it to July? I'd like to tell her myself. Once I figure out how."

"How was your coffee?" Toby looked up from his tablet and patted the space next to him on the bed.

"Hot and sweet. A lot like you, actually." June batted her eyelashes and flopped next to him.

He bumped her shoulder with his. "You know what I meant."

June chuckled and snuggled against his chest. "It was good. I wish we could do more than squeeze in an occasional Wednesday night coffee—but everyone's been so busy lately... I'll take what I can get."

"Yeah. I was thinking it's about time for Gar and me to arrange another poker night. It's been a while. Anything new?"

"She's pregnant. Almost to her second trimester."

"That's great. I'll have to shoot Kevin an email."

June pressed her lips together. Was that a good idea? "Hmm. Let me double check with Lydia. She said I could tell you, but they're keeping it quiet until they're solidly past twelve weeks."

Toby grunted. "'K. How's your project going at work?"

She bit back a groan. "Phong convinced me that he'd be able to get Henry's piece working by the end of the week. We're all going to pitch in on Jill's piece once that's set so, for better or worse, I told Bob we'd make the deadline. Good Friday is either going to be really good, or absolutely terrible."

Toby kissed the top of her head. "You'll get it done. Sounds like you've got a plan and your team's going to make it happen.

Maybe when you're finished we can take a long weekend to celebrate? Head into the mountains and hike, see the caverns?"

"If you'd asked me yesterday, I would've jumped on it. July called this afternoon—apparently Mom and Dad are coming for Easter."

Toby groaned.

"I know. And it's our turn to host. So save that getaway idea for a weekend after they come. I suspect we're both going to need a break."

"Do you think she'll remember that she decided to be okay with us adopting?"

"It's going to go one of two ways. She'll either act like adopting was her idea all along or she'll be back to thinking we're insane. There won't be any middle ground. Do you not remember my mother?"

He chuckled.

"On the other hand, July said Dad's making this into a road trip. So maybe she'll be so annoyed at him she'll leave the rest of us alone."

"There's a happy thought. Let's go with that one."

9

Toby shuffled the cards. "All right, gentlemen. Thanks for coming at such short notice. I had the idea Wednesday night and June said why not try for this week instead of some nebulous 'someday' and... here we are."

Kevin MacGregor laughed and elbowed Matt Stephenson who was sitting next to him. "I'm glad for a night out. I've been going crazy at work this week trying to prep a coworker for a multi-week trip to our India office. They wanted me to go, but that's just not feasible right now."

"Indispensable." Matt grabbed the cards Toby slid across the table. "That's my pal. Whereas I just sit in the back room of a salon twiddling my thumbs all day."

"Whatever." Kevin picked up his cards. "What about you, Gareth? Work driving you crazy? We can start a club."

Gareth chuckled and tossed a chip into the middle of the table. "Nope. The world of medical research is a pretty laid back place. At least my little pocket of it is. We're not doing anything time sensitive and, at the end of the day, I can go home and forget about things until I have to be back at work again."

"Brag, brag, brag." Toby frowned as he peeked at his cards. He tossed chips into the kitty. It was good he loved his brother-in-law. The perfect-job shtick got old. "We can still start a club, we just won't invite this loser."

"Hey." Gareth pelted Toby with a poker chip.

"Thanks, man." Toby added the chip to his own pile and dealt the next card. "Anyone else have family coming for Easter?"

Kevin and Matt exchanged glances. Both shook their head.

"Is that a thing now? Traveling for Easter?" Kevin tossed a small stack of chips into the middle to raise the bet.

"According to our mutual mother-in-law it is." Gareth tapped his cards before dropping them on the table face down. "Fold."

Toby dealt another card. "I guess we're just the lucky ones, eh, Gareth?"

"You really are. My folks and my in-laws live in town. We see them constantly. Though, honestly, both Lydia and I have a pretty decent relationship with both of them." Kevin dropped his cards to the table. "I'm out."

"Of course you have a good relationship, they're normal people. Whereas I have the joy of in-town in-laws who still suggest that I only married Laura to hide my sexual preferences. Apparently fathering three kids hasn't helped with that at all, either." Matt tossed a stack of chips on the table. "Let's see 'em, Toby."

Toby chuckled and flipped his cards. He'd forgotten about Matt's in-laws. "All right, you win." He checked the cards. Matt had three of a kind to his own two pair. "You win all around, looks like."

Grinning, Matt raked in his winnings and began organizing the chips into stacks.

The game continued for another two hours. Toby laughed as Matt told stories of crazy clients at the salon and Kevin did an amusing impression of some of his coworkers. Toby also watched Gareth out of the corner of his eye. Something was up. It wasn't likely that anyone else noticed, but they'd been friends long enough that he could see it.

After Kevin and Matt left, Toby slid the poker chip case toward Gareth and tucked the cards into their box. "What's going on with you?"

Gareth glanced up from stacking chips in the briefcase-like holder and shook his head. "Nothing."

"Gimme a break. We've been friends for ten years, brothers-in-law for seven of those years. I can tell when something's not right. Spill."

"It's nothing. I'll be fine."

"Which is it? Nothing? Or you'll be fine?" Toby began stacking red poker chips and pushing them across the table.

Gareth sighed. "June probably already told you, right?"

Toby searched his memory. June had been complaining about something to do with her sister, but he'd only half-listened, especially once she mentioned her parents were coming and that they were staying at their house this time. "She probably did. But you know how it is."

He gave a mirthless laugh. "I finally figured out that July wasn't just dragging her feet about adoption because she needed more time to get over giving up on biological children. She's just against the idea completely. Totally, one-hundred-percent against it. So I told her we'd take it off the table. You would've thought I gave her the moon."

"And... you were hoping that she'd talk you out of that gesture?"

Gareth clicked the case shut and flipped the latch. "Yeah, I guess I was. I want kids. We always talked about having a big family—that was always something I thought we both wanted. We even, ever so briefly, talked about adoption before we were married. I didn't realize she was considering it *only* as an addition to biological kids. So now... I just need to adjust."

"You need to talk to her, Gar. This isn't something you just ignore and hope you feel better about."

"Do you not remember last fall? There's no way I'm going there again. We finally have things back on a mostly level footing—totally level as far as she's concerned. I'm not rocking the boat again and getting into yet another argument with no solution that doesn't involve someone losing big time. I'll just take the hit and move on without all the arguing." Gareth pulled his keys out of his pocket. "Thanks for hosting. This was fun."

"Hey—what about talking to Pastor Brown?" Toby followed Gareth to the front door.

Gareth stepped out onto the front porch and turned, shaking his head. "What's he going to say? I need to talk to July about it, she needs to know how I feel, blah, blah, blah. Been there. Still have a crick in my back from sleeping on our guest bed because of it. It's not worth it, Tobe. But I appreciate the concern. I'll be fine."

Toby leaned against the doorframe, a sinking sensation in his gut, as Gareth got into his car and drove off. There was no way Gareth was going to just magically be fine. This was too big a difference of opinion to leave unsaid. He scratched his jaw and shut the door. Should he do something? Mention it to June? No. That was definitely not the right action. She'd turn around and tell July and they'd be in worse shape than if Gareth had brought it up himself. Pastor Brown? That wouldn't work either. Gareth would just be mad at Toby then. And, besides, Gareth had probably nailed exactly what the pastor would say. Minus the 'blah, blah' part.

Still, it was like watching two trains chugging toward each other at full speed. There was going to be a colossal crash... the only questions were when and how much damage it was going to cause. There had to be something he could do, didn't there? Toby breathed a prayer for discernment.

TOBY LOOKED up from stirring his coffee as June shuffled into the kitchen. "You got home late. Have fun?"

She nodded as she opened a cabinet and pulled out a mug. "Yeah. It's nice that July and Lydia get along too. Laura was going to try to come, but their babysitter fell through at the last minute. We headed to Laura's house after dinner and hung out for the rest of the time. It wasn't until Matt got home that we realized how late it had gotten."

"Did you leave then? I should've waited up."

June poured her coffee. "You're fine. July and I stopped for ice cream on the way home. It was almost one by the time I made it home. What about you? Poker go well?"

Toby took a long sip of coffee. "It was fun, but Matt... he's crazy. Some of the hands he won with were nuts. But it paid off for him, he took all eight bucks home."

"Ah well, there goes our summer home in Paris."

He chuckled. "Did July say anything about Gar?"

"Not really. Why?"

"He just seemed a little off. Wondered if something was up."

June pursed her lips and sat across from him at the kitchen table. "I can't think of anything. Want me to ask her?"

"Nah." That was the last thing he needed. But if July hadn't mentioned anything... should Toby talk to June? She'd keep quiet if he asked her to. What purpose would that serve though? Until he could think up a compelling argument, he'd let it rest. "So what's on our agenda for today, the last Saturday before Easter?"

She groaned. "Easter. I guess we need to make sure the house is ready for Mom and Dad."

Toby glanced around. It looked fine to him. It wasn't as if they lived like slobs. Maybe they could run the vacuum more frequently, but with just the two of them, did it really matter? "Let's save that for next weekend. The house looks great, as usual. And if your mom wants to gripe about it, she's going to do that even if we've been on a cleaning frenzy two hours before she gets here. Wanna go downtown and see the cherry blossoms? The festival started last week."

"Ugh. The crowds..."

"Oh come on. It'll be fun. It's good to get your mind off work and your parents." And Gareth.

She smiled. "All right, why not. We haven't hit up the cherry blossoms in a few years. I'll go hop in the shower."

Since the weather was nice, crowds packed the Metro. June and Toby linked hands and wound through the gawking tourists who inevitably stopped at the top of the escalator leading from the subterranean train platform to the National Mall. It was a nice view, Toby could give them that, but they could enjoy it even more if they'd take just a few steps to one side or the other. That way they weren't getting plowed into by everyone else who was hoping to take in the Washington Monument.

"Now I remember why we stopped coming down here for the blossoms." June cut across the grass toward the sidewalk that would get them to the tidal basin and the cherry trees faster.

Toby chuckled. "I was just thinking pretty much the same thing. At least we didn't try to park."

"Can you imagine? Though I suppose we could have called it a driving tour of the cherry trees and then headed back home. Kind of a waste though on such a pretty day." June bumped his hip with hers. "This was a good idea."

"Thanks." He tugged her out into the street, speeding into a shuffling run to dart between the cars that inched forward toward the red light. "Do you want to see the Jefferson, too?"

She shook her head. "Let's go find the Japanese lantern—the blossoms always seem prettier right around there. And then you can tell me what's troubling you."

Toby stifled a sigh. She could always read him so well. He hadn't said he wasn't going to mention it to June... and she'd keep it from July if he asked. It'd be hard for her, but she was getting better at it these days. Both sisters had realized that it wasn't a bad thing, now that they were grown and married, to have a few areas of their life that were off limits to the other.

"Come on, spill. I can see the gears spinning."

"I'm worried about Gareth."

June's eyebrows shot up. "Gareth? Why? Ooh—stop a minute? Isn't that just divine?"

He followed her gaze. An ethereal cloud of pale pink of the cherry blossoms clustered around the sparkling tidal pool. A light breeze lifted the blooms, sprinkling stray petals across the surface of the water. "Pretty. It's nice that the festival and the blossoms are actually happening at the same time this year. So often the blossoms are gone—or haven't started—when they've scheduled the events. The tourists actually get a treat this year."

She grinned. "True. Though I like the years when the locals get all the blooms and the tourists just get the festival. I'm greedy that way, I guess." She pulled his hand and resumed walking. "So, about Gareth?"

"You know they've put adoption on hold, permanently, from what I can gather?"

She nodded.

"He's not okay with that... it's eating at him."

"But July said he was on board. She's been elated that he took it so well." June's shoulders slumped. "You're sure?"

"Yeah. He admitted it."

"Why hasn't he said something to July?"

Toby pointed across the street. "Let's cross. The lantern is just up ahead. As far as talking to July, I asked him about that. He asked if I'd forgotten about last fall. I guess he figures at this point he has to choose between being heard and being loved."

June flinched. "That's a bit harsh, isn't it?"

"I don't know. You have to admit that July was... unpleasant... let's go with that, last fall. In the end, she got her way and I think Gareth still feels beaten up." Toby stooped to peer through the Japanese lantern at the cherry trees and tidal basin beyond. It was one of his favorite views. He'd tried to capture it with a camera once... and quickly realized he wasn't a photographer.

"She definitely didn't handle things perfectly. But... neither did Gareth."

Toby straightened. "I wasn't saying he did. He's just not in a hurry to go back there. I suggested he talk to the pastor, just on his own, but he's not interested. It worries me."

June pulled her lower lip between her teeth and nodded. "I don't think we can do anything. Just pray for them. That's a big misunderstanding to have hanging between you. Especially when one of you doesn't know it's there."

"You won't mention this to July, right?"

June scoffed. "I don't have a death wish. She's content right now, maybe even happy. Or as happy as she's going to be when it comes to children. I'm not going to be the one to burst that bubble."

Toby looked at June and smiled. When it came down to it,

he was lucky. Maybe he should say blessed, but God knew what he meant, and there was no question that having June in his life was God's doing. They had their ups and downs, but they hashed out their problems when they needed to and, as far as he could remember, hadn't stooped to emotional blackmail. "I love you."

10

Gareth flipped on the television and propped up his feet. July was up taking a nap. She'd invited him to join her, but he wasn't tired. And even though sleeping clearly hadn't been the only thing on her mind, he needed to be a little less angry before going there. Maybe he should talk to her, but there simply wasn't any way he was willing to go back to the strain of the fall. Could everyone tell something was bothering him? Well, everyone except July. She didn't seem to notice.

He wiggled his phone out of his pocket and opened a web browser. While two brothers on TV showed a young couple how they could renovate a beat-up house to make it their dream home, he played around with different search terms. He opened tabs for several promising blogs and discussion groups —maybe one of them would help.

After several minutes, Gareth had closed all but one of the likely options. Apparently, he was one of the few men in the world who was bothered by an inability to have children. Maybe that wasn't completely fair. There were a handful of men talking about their physical problems that were hindering conception. But that wasn't Gareth's problem. He was fine. Did that bother July? They'd never really talked about it. She'd say something though, wouldn't she?

Aha. This was promising—a whole discussion area for people whose partners wanted to give up. That was essentially the situation he was in. He skimmed through the subject lines, opening one here or there to read further. It seemed to be primarily women, but they were facing the same problem— they wanted to do whatever it took to have a family, their spouse was done. He browsed over to the introductions thread and composed a short introduction.

Hi –

Are men allowed to join in? My wife and I finished our second round of IVF last month. She just miscarried twins. The deal was that we'd try IVF, and if it didn't work, we'd move on to adoption. Now she's backed out and wants us to just go on with life without kids.

-G

He read it over and hit 'post,' then browsed to another thread. After several minutes, he went back to the introduction. There were several welcoming replies, all expressing how unfair July's behavior was and encouraging him to share more. Gareth pursed his lips. What more was there to say?

July shuffled in, rubbing her eyes. "Hey. What'cha watching?"

Gareth's gaze flicked to the TV. "It was those brothers. Now...I don't know what this is. Doesn't look familiar."

She glanced at his phone. "Work?"

"Nah. Just browsing online." His stomach twisted. It was as close to a lie as he'd ever told July. But if he admitted what he was doing, they'd have to get into a discussion of why, and that'd open the whole can of worms. Not worth it. He clicked off his phone and tucked it back into his pocket. "Was there something you wanted to watch?"

"WHEN YOU GET TO WORK, can you check how much vacation you've got available? I was thinking we could plan a trip for this summer. Maybe finally head overseas. I've been getting a discount travel email the past several weeks—they've got some great deals to Ireland." July brought her coffee to the kitchen table and sat across from him.

Now she wanted to travel? When they were dating, traveling had been her dream. He hadn't initially been interested in that, but over time, she'd swayed him to her side. They'd had to save up for a bit, get settled with their jobs, but when they'd hit the point where it was reasonable, he'd tried to get her to travel. Of course by then, it seemed as if she'd moved on to being gung ho about starting a family. He'd taken some convincing to get on that train, too. But he'd finally seen the benefits of being younger parents. And now... what? She was swinging back to travel and expecting him to fall in line like he had the past two times? He grunted a response. Let her take it however she wanted to. He'd check his vacation days, but no matter how much he'd wanted to travel before, it was going to take more than a great deal on airfare to get him to go for that.

"You okay?"

He shrugged. "Monday, you know?"

She pursed her lips and watched him over the top of her mug. He could practically hear the wheels turning as she tried to decide whether or not she should push him. After several minutes of silence she sighed and drained her coffee. "I'm going to run. I've got meetings all afternoon, so any actual work I want to get done needs to happen this morning. I may be late getting home—it's going to depend on the meetings. You know how it is, we're getting close to April 15th."

Gareth nodded. This was nothing new. Marriage to an accountant had its periods of insanity and then periods of normalcy. Much like anything, probably. At least with accountants it was somewhat predictable. "Okay. Have a good day."

"Love you." July kissed the top of his head, grabbed her laptop bag, and hurried out the kitchen door to the garage.

Her car's engine growled as she backed down the driveway. He thumbed on his phone and browsed to the discussion forum, a smile tugging at his lips. Some of the commentary the other members posted was hilarious. At least they were able to find the humor in their predicament. He hadn't managed that yet. A blinking envelope at the top of his screen caught his eye. A private message? He opened it and skimmed. A woman, Holly, wanted to know how to suggest adoption to her husband. She said she was looking for a logical breakdown of the pros and cons that would convince a typical man. That was easy. He hit reply and started typing.

11

July closed the folder and tucked it into her desk drawer. One tax return ready for signatures and filing. Far-too-many-to-count left to go. Those weren't likely to be addressed today though, not with meetings that were bound to be a waste of time scheduled for the afternoon. Maybe some people appreciated the rah-rah to gear up for the IRS deadline push, but she'd just as soon close the door and get some work done. She could feel good about her job when it was finished.

Her stomach growled. The coffee she'd had for breakfast wasn't holding her... maybe June could use a break, too. She shot her sister a text and rummaged through her purse for her wallet. She hadn't remembered to pack food today, so she was going to have to run out for something anyway. Sliding her phone into her pocket, she strode toward the elevators.

July's phone buzzed as she crossed the courtyard. Sweet. June would be down in ten. That gave her time to grab a sandwich and stake out a bench. It was a semi-dreary day for late March. They'd probably get some rain later this afternoon, if the clouds were any indication. At least she'd have something to look at out the conference room window.

Tucking the bag from the deli under her arm, July unwrapped a straw and poked it into her soda as she hurried back toward the courtyard. There was one bench getting a few anemic beams of sunlight through a break in the clouds. She angled for it, staking her claim just ahead of a group of workers.

June dashed across the pavement. "Sorry. Bob caught me just as I was hitting the elevator. That man... I don't know what it's going to take to convince him we really are going to meet our deadline. Though it'd be helpful if I believed that a bit more fervently. There's a chance we will... but it's slim. Friday's going to be here before I know what hit me."

"And with it, Mom and Dad. You ready?" July tore the plastic off her sandwich and took a bite.

June shrugged. "As ready as I'm going to be. There're clean sheets on the guest bed. Beyond that... they'll just have to take what they get. Toby refuses to get worked up about it and I have to say it's refreshing not being wound up about it. How's your workload? You ready for it to be April?"

"No." July groaned. "Everyone's taking their sweet time getting me what I need this year. I've already started filling out extension request paperwork for two of my clients. They haven't said they're not going to be on time, but if they keep up the way they've been all year, they'll drop the files off on the fourteenth and wonder why I'm annoyed."

June chuckled. "I could sic Bob on them, if you wanted."

"Don't tempt me." July flipped up the top piece of bread and eyed the fixings. There were pickles... she'd said no pickles. She picked off the wilted green circles and dropped them on the wrapper. "What'd you and Toby do on Saturday?"

July half listened as June rambled on about the cherry blossoms and the museums they'd wandered through when they were finished outside. "What about you?"

"Us? We just hung out around home. I mentioned a few things, but Gareth didn't seem interested. In fact... I practically had to kick him out of the house to make him go to poker on Friday. Did Toby say anything about him acting weird?"

June's eyebrows arched up. "What do you mean?"

"I don't know. He just seems... off. Wondered if Toby had noticed it or if it was just me. Maybe I'm reading into things." July dropped the uneaten portion of her lunch back onto the plastic wrap. "I asked him about maybe planning a trip overseas this summer and only got a grunt. I've been dying to go abroad for years, but now that it might be feasible he's not even a teeny bit excited?"

"Men are weird." June balled up her trash, her eyes darting to the side. "Have you asked him?"

July sighed. "Not yet. I was kind of hoping to get some insight before I did that. I usually have some idea what's going on, but this time? No clue. I hate going in blind."

"Sorry." June stood. "I should get back before Bob starts looking for me and terrorizes my team. Right now they've got their heads down and they're coding away. But if he starts in on them... we'll never make Friday."

BACK IN HER OFFICE, July dialed in to the teleconference, put her speakerphone on mute, and opened her email. She listened with half an ear as the main office droned on about client satisfaction and remembering to take breaks and exercise during this, the busiest time of the year. She could probably give this speech verbatim if she tried.

She clicked through a travel website ad and scanned the airfare deals. Two weeks in England... they could do a lot of sightseeing in that amount of time. But it wasn't so long that they'd start missing home. Two weeks with nothing to do but reconnect. It'd be like their daytrip to Annapolis... just longer. Her mouse hovered over the button to purchase. Gareth should have enough vacation time available. When was the last time either of them had taken more than a couple of days off? But his schedule... if he was in the middle of a test protocol that couldn't go on without him... she groaned. Better wait until she got some dates from him. July copied the URL and shot an email to Gareth asking what he thought. England—well, all of the British Isles—had always been high on his list of places to see. Surely that'd pop him out of his funk. What was eating at him? It wasn't like him to keep quiet when something was wrong. She sighed. There was nothing she could do about it right now.

She opened a client file and started going through a checklist. The speaker on the call had switched, but the rhetoric was still the same. Rah-rah, do those taxes. Sheesh. Just hang up and let us get to work. July composed a quick email reminding the client of the three missing items that were necessary for her to be able to complete the filing and switched to the next folder in her stack. Maybe she'd be able to get some work done during the meeting after all.

"Honey, I'm home." July kicked off her shoes and dropped her bag by the door. The kitchen light was on, but nothing else. Where was he? "Gareth? You home?"

She poked her head in each room as she made her way upstairs. Sure, she'd told him she'd be late, but usually when he made plans he let her know. "Gar?"

She padded into the bedroom. Gareth lay stretched out on the bed, laptop balanced on his stomach, headphones on. That explained the lack of response. She leaned in to kiss him.

He jolted and snapped the lid of his computer shut then

tugged off his headphones. "Hey. You're earlier than I expected."

July perched next to him on the side of the bed. "Yeah. I managed to get some preliminary stuff done during the meeting. So I called it a day. Did you eat?"

"Not yet. I wasn't hungry, so I figured I'd wait until either I wanted something or you got home." He cocked his head to the side. "You hungry?"

She was. But she didn't really want to cook. "Sandwich?"

"Sure. Want me to fix it?"

She grinned. "Would you? You're the best. Even PB&J is fine."

Gareth pushed off the bed and tucked his laptop under his arm. "I'll see what we've got."

July watched him disappear. Something was definitely up. Why'd he close his laptop and take it with him? Maybe he just didn't want to forget where he left it. But still... it wasn't as if she cared what he was doing on it. She trusted him, just like he trusted her. Neither of them worried about things like that. She shrugged out of her work clothes and pulled on her pajamas before padding downstairs.

Gareth flipped sandwiches in a skillet. "Grilled cheese okay? I know you said peanut butter..."

"That's even better. I was trying to minimize effort. Thanks." July flopped into a chair at the table. "How was your day?"

"Nothing spectacular. Martin's leaving."

She wracked her brain but came up blank. "Remind me who Martin is."

"Mmm. So skinny he looks emaciated, always wears a plaid tie." He scooped the sandwiches onto plates and cut them in half before carrying them to the table. "Brought his morbidly obese girlfriend to the Christmas party."

She chuckled as the picture of the couple swam into her memory. "Oh. Jack Sprat and his wife."

"That's Martin. They are, in fact, getting married—in August, I think. Her job's moving her to Boston though, so he found a new position up there. Not sure doing what. But they're going to move up in May, so he put his notice in today."

"Will that impact any of your work?" If they were going to be short-handed, could he even get vacation time? July watched the vision of their vacation overseas fly off into the sunset, leaving them behind on the runway.

Gareth bit into his sandwich. "Shouldn't. We were running staff-heavy anyway. Losing one or two shouldn't cause problems. Just means a tad less downtime for the rest of us. Speaking of which, I have about a month of vacation saved up. So if you want to do the overseas thing, we could."

If she wanted to? Didn't he want to? "What's wrong? I thought you'd be excited about this. Last year, traveling was all you could talk about and now it's if I want to?"

"People change their minds about things. You should know that." He scooted back from the table, leaving a half-eaten sandwich on his plate. "I think I'm going to go for a walk."

She blinked, unable to summon a coherent sentence, as he stuffed his feet into his sneakers, grabbed his cell phone, and strode out the door. If he didn't want to go abroad she wasn't going to force him...but this felt bigger than vacation planning. Clearly, she was missing something.

12

G areth thumbed on his phone and tapped out a post in the "Can You Believe This?!?" thread of the discussion group. Was July really that clueless? She'd even said "last year." How was she not making the connection to *before* all this baby madness? He could admit that originally he'd been the one reminding her that they had plenty of time. He'd even tried to tempt her into waiting with her dreams of travel, reminding her that they should do it before they were tied down with kids. But after the first miscarriage... having seen the baby on the ultrasound machine... that changed everything. He'd gone from wanting kids at some point to wanting them now. While they were young enough to enjoy them. Maybe he hadn't wanted to do all the craziness of IVF, but she'd had her heart set on it. Plus, she'd promised they'd look into adoption if it didn't work. Doing fifteen minutes worth of research on the Internet didn't count. Point being, they'd end up with children one way or another. He didn't care which way. Not having kids wasn't something they'd ever discussed. Let alone agreed on.

He slowed, focusing on his breathing and calming his

heartbeat. A tiny voice in the back of his head—one that sounded an awful lot like Toby—suggested that he needed to be talking to July about this, not online strangers. But July wasn't going to understand. At best, she'd ask him why he hadn't said something immediately and then discount the fact that he was annoyed now because he hadn't spoken up. At worst... they'd be back to sleeping in separate rooms and talking around each other. As much as he wanted to believe they'd learned more about communicating when they met with the pastor... the fact that she could go back on her word so quickly kind of killed it for him. After all, if you were committed to a relationship, didn't you at least try to pretend you cared about how your husband felt? If you loved someone, didn't you sometimes do things that weren't what you wanted because it was important to the other? That's certainly the only reason he'd agreed to IVF. But it was clear the road didn't go both ways.

He rounded the corner of the block. The porch light shone in the distance like a beacon. But a beacon of what? He didn't want a divorce. That just simply wasn't something he'd consider. He'd made his choice and now... he was stuck with July for better or for worse. He didn't want to talk about how he was feeling either. That was just opening a can of worms that needed to stay shut. There was no way to win. But he didn't want to be childless, either. Which left him to choose which of the three things he didn't want that he'd be able to live with.

As he approached their yard, his phone signaled a new private message in the discussion forum. He laughed aloud at Holly's first line. At least someone understood. He sent a quick reply before heading back inside to face the music.

JULY WAS LOUNGING IN BED, reading. She didn't look up when he came in the room. Great. The ice wall was up. Maybe she'd thaw if he apologized straight off. He cleared his throat.

"I'm sorry I took off."

She let her e-reader drop onto her lap and looked at him.

He fought a sigh. Was he going to have to grovel? "I guess I'm still adjusting to the idea that we're just giving up on kids all together. All this talk of traveling... it's what you do when you don't have any ties at home. It just makes it more real."

That was true, as far as it went. And it was, hopefully, resigned enough to keep her from erupting at him. It still sounded like he was okay with it, right?

July gave a short nod. "Don't storm off again, please? We can't work things out if you don't stay to talk about it. That whole mess this fall... that all started because I closed myself off to you. I really don't want to go there again."

He almost snorted at the irony. She closed herself off and caused the mess, but now if he didn't back away they'd be in a fight that would make the fall look like a day at the circus. "Me either."

"You coming to bed?"

The tension in his gut uncoiled as he saw the invitation in her eyes. At least he hadn't bungled things badly enough that they were going to end up embroiled in an argument all night. He nodded. "Let me go brush my teeth."

13

T oby compared the contents of his shopping cart with the list June had texted him at lunch. Stopping at the grocery store on his way home from work wasn't high on his list of fun activities, but with her parents showing up tomorrow—or possibly Saturday, depending on how their road trip was going—June was getting anxious. With this out of the way, they should be set. And he might just put his foot down if she tried to do more frantic cleaning. They might be her parents, but she was an adult. Theoretically, they should love her no matter how many dust bunnies lived under the sofa and, at this point, she shouldn't need their approval anyway. Of course, that only worked in self-help books. In reality, everyone appeared to continue to struggle to find that balance of adult interaction and respecting the familial requirements. He and his parents still hit bumps... just not to quite the same degree as June. But then, her parents were unique.

He pushed the cart into an open checkout lane and began unloading. His cell rang. "Hello?"

"Hey, it's Gareth. Got a minute?"

Toby glanced between the cart, the conveyor belt, and the

cashier. "Can you give me five? I'll call you back when I'm done at the grocery store."

"Sure. Yeah, that's great."

Frowning, he stuck the phone in his pocket. There had been tinges of something... panic, maybe, in Gareth's voice. He stared, unseeing, at the cash register readout as the lady scanned his goods. Maybe Gar was finally ready to admit he needed to talk to someone. That'd be a good thing. He swiped his credit card and signed the keypad when the total blinked. Shaking his head, he took the last bag and smiled at the cashier. "Thanks, have a good day."

Toby dropped the bag into the cart and fished his phone out of his pocket while he angled across the parking lot to his car.

"Hey man, what's up?"

Gareth cleared his throat. "What are you doing tonight?"

Clamping the phone to his ear with his shoulder, Toby popped open the trunk lid and began transferring bags of groceries. "I don't know—probably helping June with whatever last minute project she's dreamed up to impress her parents. Her latest idea was to get the guest room all done up like a nursery, since it'll be the nursery at some point. I managed to convince her that would only give Mom permission to pester her about adoption the whole time they were here. Plus, it's not as if she wanted a neutral scheme. So if we end up with a boy instead of a girl then what? We have to redecorate like mad? Uh-uh. Sorry... why?"

"I forgot they were coming this weekend... never mind."

"Nope, tell me." Toby slammed the trunk and pushed the cart toward the corral a few spots down.

"Okay. I was thinking I might go to this infertility support group and they're meeting tonight. But... I didn't really want to go on my own. I'm worried I'll be the only guy there, even though Holly said that wouldn't matter. Still."

Toby furrowed his brow. A support group sounded like a positive step. Maybe. "July didn't want to go with you?"

Silence stretched over the line. "I haven't told her about it."

"You've gotta tell her, man. I was hoping the group was because you'd had a conversation."

"So you won't come then?" A hard edge crept into Gareth's tone.

"I didn't say that. Text me the details. I'll double check with June that she doesn't need me and let you know. I have to at least get the groceries home."

"Okay."

Toby started the engine and pointed the car toward home. What was Gareth thinking, not even mentioning it to July? Did he think she'd object? Or was it that he didn't want her to know he was unhappy with how things were going right now?

"THAT'S THE LAST BAG." Toby set the plastic sack on the counter and tucked his hands in his pockets. "What did you have planned for tonight?"

June seemed to shrink in on herself. "Some fretting, which I'll possibly do curled up in the fetal position. Maybe some moaning. I hadn't decided for sure on that one yet."

Chuckling, Toby moved behind her and rubbed her shoulders. "It's not that bad, is it? They've stayed with us before."

"I know. This time I have this feeling of foreboding, like something terrible is going to happen."

He dropped his chin on top of her head and she leaned back against him, gradually relaxing. "It's going to be all right. And if we have to, we'll drive them over to Gareth and July's and leave them there."

June snickered.

"Speaking of Gareth..."

She twisted around and looked up at him. "Why do I feel like I need to say 'uh-oh'?"

Toby linked his hands around her waist. "Because you have good instincts. He's thinking of going to an infertility support group tonight... wondered if I would go along."

"July's not going?"

He chuckled. At least her response proved he wasn't completely off base in thinking that it was more of a couple's thing. Or should be. "She doesn't even know he wants to go."

June groaned. "Where'd he hear about it?"

"Dunno. I didn't ask—he got annoyed when I asked why July wasn't going along."

"Go." June shook her head and pulled away. "He needs someone sane with him."

Toby kissed her forehead then her lips. "You're sure you'll be okay? I don't want to miss out on quality moaning."

"I'll save that part of the program for when you get home." June waggled her eyebrows.

He let out a snorting laugh. "You really can't pull off the libidinous wench look, you know that, right?"

June swatted at him. "Get out of here. Call me when you're on your way home."

Toby pulled into a parking spot outside the cozy, hole-in-the-wall, Italian restaurant. He glanced over at Gareth. "Isn't this an odd place for a support group?"

"I guess. It's another reason why, after Holly sent me the directions, I thought it might be good for you to tag along."

"Tell me about this Holly person. You've mentioned her a couple of times now."

Gareth crossed his arms and shifted in the passenger seat of Toby's car. "She's just someone from the online forums I've been visiting. We've got a lot in common—her husband is totally against adoption and she feels like he led her on during fertility treatment. Now she doesn't know what to do, because he expects them to just go on about their life without kids. Sound familiar?"

Alarm bells sounded in Toby's brain. He cleared his throat. "And has she talked to her husband about it?"

"She says he just blows up, so she's given up trying."

Toby frowned. His brother-in-law wasn't usually stupid, but how did he not see the glaring problems with this situation? "So he won't be here tonight?"

Gareth shook his head.

"Anyone else from these forums going to be here tonight?"

"Not that I know of. Holly said it was just a handful of people she'd met at her doctor's office and that sort of thing. Nothing really formal, but a good place to commiserate."

Toby scrubbed a hand over his face. "Well, let's go see."

Gareth unclipped his seatbelt and headed for the restaurant. Toby followed behind. He couldn't come up with any positive outcomes for this group. If there even was a group. But Gareth was in such a weird place right now, saying something was probably not going to be useful. He'd just let it play out.

The mostly-deserted restaurant was dimly lit, primarily by candles that flickered in Chianti bottles on each table. A long wooden bar stretched down the left side of the space. A lone middle-aged woman dressed like a teenager, complete with bare midriff and too-tight skirt, perched on a stool, a glass of red wine at her elbow. Gareth stood at the hostess stand, looking around.

Toby tucked his hands in his pockets and stopped behind Gareth, trying to look like an unrelated customer. "Did she say where the group meets? Maybe there's a banquet room in the back?"

Gareth shook his head. "She said it wasn't crowded and I'd see her. It's not crowded, that's for sure but..."

"Maybe at the bar?" Toby fought the urge to grimace. If that was Holly, this was even worse than he'd anticipated.

The hostess appeared from the back of the restaurant. "Two?"

"No, I'm looking for a group—the coordinator is Holly?"

"That's Holly at the bar, she's a regular. Not sure about any group though." The hostess looked beyond Gareth and caught Toby's eyes. "Just one?"

"Actually, can I see a menu first?"

Sighing, the hostess slapped a menu down on the stand and huffed. "Let me know when you're ready to be seated."

Toby shot Gareth a look as the hostess stomped off. "I'll wait here."

Confusion written across his face, Gareth crossed to the woman on the stool. Toby scooted to the end of the bar and leaned against it, letting his eyes roam over the menu, his ears straining to hear the conversation.

"Holly?"

A broad grin, full of invitation, split the woman's face. "You must be Gareth. I'm so glad you came."

"Where's the rest of the group?"

The woman's grin slipped into a sly smile and she patted the stool next to her. "No one else could make it. Why don't you sit down and have a drink?"

"Um. That's okay. When... when's the next meeting scheduled?" Gareth shuffled back a step and stuffed his hands in his pockets.

"Whenever you want it to be. What's good for you?" Holly leaned forward. Even from the other end of the bar, her assets loomed large.

Red burned across Gareth's cheeks. "I... I... I'm going to go."

"Don't run off."

Shaking his head, Gareth turned on his heel and strode from the restaurant. Toby waited until the door slapped shut behind him before following.

"Hey. Hold up." Toby jogged to catch up. "You all right?"

Gareth shook his head.

"Want to talk about it?"

"Not really. Let's just go home. Okay?"

Gareth stared out the passenger window. At least Toby wasn't pushing it. Was it possible to feel like a bigger idiot? No. No, it really wasn't. And no one was going to believe he hadn't realized there was no support group. Holly seemed so normal, so understanding, in the discussion forum. The fact that she lived in the area just happened to be a bonus. But if there wasn't really a group... had she even gone through all the stuff she talked about? She certainly didn't look like a woman who was upset about not having kids. If the hostess hadn't pointed him that way, he would have assumed she was a working girl they tolerated for some unknown reason. He sighed.

"Are you going to tell July?"

"Tell her what?" Gareth turned to look at Toby.

Toby kept his gaze fixed on the road. "You don't think she needs to know what almost happened back there?"

"Nothing almost happened. I went to a restaurant, realized I made a mistake, and then went home. End of story." Almost happened. Please. Toby was blowing this way out of proportion.

"Or, you made a friend online and agreed to meet her. I'm just surprised you wanted me along."

"Look. I didn't know there wasn't a group. Maybe that makes me stupid and gullible, I don't know. The fact of the matter is I never gave Holly any reason to believe that I'd cheat on July, because I wouldn't. I just wanted someone to talk to who would understand without making it into a big argument that ended up with me being the bad guy." Gareth raked a hand through his hair and turned back to stare out the window.

"And the fact that you had to do any of that is why you need to talk to July."

Gareth frowned. Toby might be right, but it still wasn't a conversation he was interested in having. "Maybe."

Toby scoffed but otherwise remained silent for the rest of the drive. He pulled into Gareth's driveway and shifted the car into park.

"Look man, I get that you're going through some stuff. But if you can't talk to July, you need to talk to someone you can trust. Not online strangers. Promise me you'll call Pastor Brown. Please?"

Gareth pushed open the door. "Thanks for driving me."

"Gar."

He shook his head. It wasn't something he could promise. Talking to Pastor Brown was just going to get him another conversation about how he needed to talk to July. But there was no point in talking to July if she wasn't going to listen. "How about this? I promise not to agree to meet anyone from the Internet in person again. That work?"

Toby's shoulders drooped. "If that's the best I can get, I'll take it. But I'm going to keep praying that you come to your senses and talk to your wife."

Gareth forced a smile. "Okay. Thanks again."

He watched Toby back out of the driveway. His taillights had faded into the distance before he turned and stared at the house. His feet were rooted to the ground. July would want to talk about where he'd been and how Toby was, and he didn't have the energy. Hiding the online forums wasn't hard. He did all that on his phone. But he'd had to make up a story to get out of the house. He hadn't misled her, exactly. And he certainly hadn't lied. He just let her believe her version of things. Even in his head, it sounded weak. But what choice did he have? He'd just need to avoid a long conversation about the evening. No point wading in any deeper than he already was.

With a breath to steady his quivering stomach, he crossed to the porch and pushed open the door.

"ARE you sure we shouldn't be helping June and Toby?" Gareth stretched out on the sofa, TV remote in his hand.

July nestled against him and shook her head. "Mom and Dad aren't going to make it 'til tomorrow now, probably late for that matter. I still can't believe Dad talked Mom into this crazy road trip. Or that Mom convinced Dad to dip south and see Charleston since they were driving all over creation anyway. Those are her words, by the way."

Gareth chuckled. Of course Betty could get Ed to do whatever she wanted. But why would Ed want to spend that much time in the car alone with Betty? Though they'd been married long enough... maybe you could get used to anything. "Well, since it's unlikely they'll do this again in their lifetime, I guess it's good they're hitting all the places Mom wanted to go. Right?"

"I guess. I was kind of looking forward to seeing them. Since they aren't staying with us." She nudged him with her elbow as his phone buzzed in his pocket. "Is that your cell?"

"Yeah, sorry. Forgot it was in there." He fished it out and set it on the cushion behind his head.

"Do you need to get it?"

"Nah. Probably an email from work. I'll look later. What are we watching?"

July snuggled back in. "It was your turn to choose. I'm game for whatever."

"Let's browse. If you see something, holler." He flipped to their streaming service and began to scroll. The phone behind his head buzzed again. He needed to remember to turn off mobile alerts for the new discussion board he'd joined. After the disaster the night before with Holly and her fake support group, he'd deleted his account on that board and poked around for somewhere else to vent. Neither of the top options seemed as welcoming as the first board, but he certainly wasn't going back there.

"Ooh, let's watch that." July tapped his hand as he scrolled.

Chick flick. So much for it being his turn to choose. He hit play and set down the remote. Could he check his phone, adjust the settings, without July noticing? He glanced down to her head resting on his chest. She was already engrossed and it was just the opening credits. He eased the phone into his hand and turned it on. Text messages? Whose number was that?

He skimmed the texts, his chest tightening. How had Holly gotten his phone number? He hadn't told her his last name. Had he mentioned July's name? Gareth and July were an odd enough combination... his stomach sank. He swiped open his browser and typed their names, along with Maryland, into the search engine. There was enough information there to piece it together if you wanted to take the time to do so. Holly apparently did. He let out a breath, willing his heart to slow. Now what?

"You all right?"

He held the power button on his phone, shutting it down, and dropped it on the cushion. "Yeah. Yeah, I'm fine. Just a wrong number text. Someone looking for a party."

July snickered. "Ah, the good old days."

He smiled. Right. Like they'd ever been ones to party. At least she seemed to believe him. Of course she did. He'd never given her a reason not to. Until now. His insides coiled into a tight ball. There was nothing wrong with talking to someone about his struggles, was there? Of course not. The lie twisted the knot in his stomach tighter. Whatever. He was just saving himself some trouble. July wasn't any more excited about fighting over kids than he was. It was better for both of them if they didn't have that conversation. He swallowed the acid that crept up his throat. Who was he kidding?

What was he supposed to do now?

15

June punched the button to turn on the oven light and peered at the ham. Honey-glaze bubbled across its surface. Almost ready. She grabbed the sheet tray holding asparagus and gave it a gentle shake. Oil, salt, and pepper coated the bright green spears. Her mouth watered as she slid them into the oven on the top rack. July was bringing yeast rolls, so the simple but festive meal would be complete as soon as they arrived. An éclair cake was chilling in the fridge for dessert. Her mother would complain. It was inevitable. Too simple? Not enough variety? One of those. Of course, had she gone all out and created a magnificent spread of delights, her mother would have chastised her for spending so much time and money buying exotic ingredients for a family meal. She was never going to win... why did it still bother her so much?

She wiped her hands on the apron tied around her waist and turned, smacking into Toby.

"Table's set and it smells delicious in here. Anything else I can do to help?"

June shook her head. "We're just waiting on July and

Gareth. Everything's basically ready to go. What are Mom and Dad doing?"

"Resting." He pulled her into his arms and kissed her. "Apparently the sunrise service wasn't what they'd had in mind for their Easter celebration."

"Great. They're going to fall asleep and we'll have to hold lunch. Of course, Gareth and July are already late... you're sure they're coming?"

Toby squeezed then released her. "They'll be here. Your parents are just lying down for a few minutes. I have strict instructions to get them as soon as your sister gets here. It's going to be fine... why are you so wound up?"

June groaned. "I don't know. I can't stop thinking about last Thanksgiving."

"When we visited them?"

"No. When they were here last. It's not as if I've lost any weight—and I really want some of that cake. The tiny snitch I took of the cream filling was so good. Plus, we still don't have a baby, nor are we actively doing anything about it. And with Gareth and July giving up all together... I feel like we're tiptoeing through a mine field. One wrong step and ka-boom, body parts start flying everywhere."

Toby laughed. "It's going to be okay. I'll go text Gareth and see what's holding them up."

June rubbed the back of her neck as he left. Was she borrowing trouble? Granted, her parents had been relatively normal yesterday when they'd arrived. But they'd also been tired from the long drive. Mom had made a few snippy comments on the way to the sunrise service. Again, maybe Mom was just tired but... the sense of foreboding just wouldn't go away. Waiting just made it worse. Was it possible Mom'd pick on July this time around?

As much as Mom wasn't completely excited about their decision to adopt, at least they were working toward providing her with grandchildren. July and Gareth had completely stopped. That was the last she'd heard anyway. Toby had been tight-lipped about the support group on Thursday night. They hadn't been gone very long, either. Had it not gone well? No one was there? June had tried to find out but Toby just shook his head and told her to pray for Gareth. If there was something bigger going on there, Mom was sure to pick up on it.

"Sorry we're late. I didn't think there'd be traffic on Easter." July set a bowl covered with a pink and green checked dishtowel on the island. "Where are Mom and Dad?"

"Right here, dear." Betty fluffed her hair as she entered the kitchen and swept July into a hug. "Dad and I wanted to rest before lunch. Did you go to a different church this morning?"

July shook her head. "No. But I can't talk Gareth—or myself —into the sunrise service. We hit up the nine o'clock and then battled traffic home to make the rolls. I thought for sure the roads would clear up but traffic was even worse on the way over here. That's why we're late. Sorry."

"Oh, don't be. It's not as if your sister has lunch ready to go." Betty turned to June. "How much longer will it be?"

The oven timer buzzed and June snapped her mouth shut on a sharp retort. She should've known Mom wasn't going to pick on July. "Everything's ready. Why don't you all go have a seat in the dining room? July, could you gather the guys and take the rolls in?"

When the kitchen was clear, June pulled out the asparagus and slid it into a serving bowl, then transferred the ham to a platter. She carved off several slices but left the rest for people to cut their own. Dad would want to cut his extra thick. Mom... would complain no matter what she did, so why bother trying to please her?

The phone rang. Who'd be calling on Easter? June ignored it and balanced the bowl of asparagus in the crook of her arm, leaving her both hands to carry the ham. The answering machine clicked on.

"Hi June and Toby, it's Faith. Could you give me a call as soon as possible?" She rattled off her cell number then hung up.

June froze. Why was Faith calling? Was there... could there be...? Her thoughts were a jumbled mess. Gradually, the searing heat from the bowl against the inside of her elbow jumpstarted her heart. She hurried into the dining room and set down the food, her gaze searching out Toby. Had he heard the machine?

He lifted his brows and nodded to her seat at the end of the table. Clearly, he hadn't heard. Should she...

"June, dear. Have a seat so we can pray and eat. Or did you need to go get the rest of the meal?"

She sighed and looked at her mother. "This is everything. Unless we need butter and jam for the rolls?"

July shook her head. "We shouldn't. I put on a sweet butter glaze."

"Well." Betty eyed the sparse table. "Plain fare is always nice, too. If a tad less celebratory than one might expect."

Ed nudged her with his elbow and frowned. "It looks—and smells—delicious."

June managed a faint smile as she tugged out her chair. Her eyes met Toby's, his look full of questions. She gave a slight shake of her head.

"Dad, would you do the honor?" Toby smiled at Ed.

"Love to."

Everyone bowed their head and Ed said a short prayer of thanksgiving. As 'Amens' worked their way around the table, June gestured toward the bowls. "Help yourself to whatever's closest. Toby? Could you help me in the kitchen for a second?"

The clatter of silverware pinged into the kitchen from the

dining room. It would, most likely, drown out their conversation.

"What's up? You okay?"

"I don't know... listen." June punched the play button on the answering machine and Faith's brief message spilled into the room. "Should we call now?"

Toby was already dialing. He tipped the handset away from his ear slightly. June scooted closer and leaned so she could hear.

"This is Faith."

"Hi, Faith. It's Toby and June."

Muffled voices carried over the line. Where was Faith?

"Oh, I'm so glad you called me back. I'm at Fairfax Hospital. A woman gave birth early yesterday morning and wants to place the baby. When she told me what she was hoping for in parents for the child, I thought of you. She's seen your portfolio and says that if you're willing to come today, she wants you. They'll be discharging her in a few hours, she wants the baby to go home with her new parents."

June's gaze locked with Toby's. Her? A girl? They had a baby girl? The breath caught in her throat and blood pounded in her ears. Tears spilled down her cheeks and she erupted in near-hysterical laughter.

Toby cleared his throat. "Yeah. Yes. Of course. We'll... we'll leave right away."

"Wonderful. I'll let the birthmother know and text you the details. If you get in touch when you park, I'll meet you in the lobby."

"Right. Sure. Um. We'll see you soon." Toby clicked end and looked at June, mouth agape. "Did that... are we... ?"

June nodded. "Either that or we're both having the same surreal hallucination."

"Go get your purse. And the camera. Don't forget the camera." Toby paused. "Car seat. We don't have a car seat."

"We'll stop on the way." She threw her arms around Toby and pressed her lips to his before dashing upstairs.

June splashed water on her face, dried it, and patted on some powder. Should she change her clothes? She eyed her outfit. It was clean, thanks to the apron she'd worn while she cooked, but casual. Should she dress up? But then she'd have to convince Toby to dress up. That wasn't going to happen. This would do. She skipped back downstairs.

"June? The food's getting cold. Where are you?" Her mother's irritated voice rang through the house.

Why hadn't Toby told them? She popped her head in the dining room and cleared her throat. "Actually... there's been a slight change of plans. Toby and I need to run. Faith, from the adoption agency, just called. There was a baby born yesterday, ready to be discharged, and the birthmother wants us."

Betty pushed her chair back and started to rise. "I'll go grab my purse. Come on, Ed."

June's jaw dropped. She wasn't seriously going to try and come, was she? Of course she was.

Ed put a hand on Betty's leg and pushed her back into her seat. "This isn't about us, Betty. Sit down and eat. You two run on now and text us a photo as soon as you have one."

"Thanks, Dad." June kissed the top of his head and leaned over to squeeze her mother's stiff shoulders. "July, there's a cake in the fridge when everyone's finished. I was going to make coffee..."

"Go. I can figure it out." July's smile lacked warmth and didn't reach her eyes. But that was something to worry about later.

Toby set his hand on her shoulder. "Ready, June?"

She nodded. "Let's go."

16

The food in July's stomach congealed into a concrete mass. The skin on her face was tight as she forced her lips into a smile. Dry eyes burned as she choked back hysterical screams. "Who's ready for cake?"

She escaped into the kitchen and stuck her head into the fridge. The cold air soothed the heat that flooded her face. A baby. Her sister was having a baby. Adoption had been a nebulous concept filled with "maybe" and "at some point" and "hopefully." Now? Now it was real. She stared, unseeing, at the contents of June's fridge.

"It's great, isn't it?" Gareth wrapped his arms around her from behind and rested his cheek on her head.

July swallowed. That wasn't in the top hundred words she'd choose, but it was certainly the expected answer. "Yeah... great. Could you figure out the coffee?"

Gareth's arms tightened around her before releasing. July kept her face in the fridge and took a deep breath. She couldn't break down here. Not with everyone around. No one would understand. Mom would talk about how July should be happy for her sister—probably the same speech she gave June when

July'd gotten pregnant so easily. Dad would assume she was hormonal. And Gar? He'd probably see that as some kind of glimmer of hope that she'd change her mind about adopting. After all, it hadn't taken that long for June and Toby and she'd used the timeframe as one of her excuses. A tear slipped down her cheek and she quickly scrubbed it away with her shoulder and reached for the éclair cake. It looked good—lots of chocolate and thick pastry cream. Maybe she could eat enough to end up in a sugar coma and not have to deal with this for another few days.

July bumped the fridge closed with her hip and set the cake pan down on the counter. "How's the coffee going?"

"Brewing away. Need help with anything else?"

She shook her head as she peeled back the plastic wrap.

"You okay?" Concern flickered in his eyes.

Could she be honest? She had to try. "I don't know. I will be... I guess maybe I'm in shock?"

Gareth drew his brows together. "But it's a good kind of shock, right? You're happy for them?"

"Of course." July forced a smile and slid a piece of cake onto a plate. It wasn't a complete lie. There was a huge ball of emotion ping-ponging around inside her. Happy was one element. But he wasn't going to understand. Gareth had never wrapped his head around her ability to mix emotions—he was a very black and white kind of guy. It must make life so much easier to be that way. "Let's get this served. Then maybe we can find a movie to watch or something while we wait."

"Should we go home? Just leave Mom and Dad here alone?" July leaned against the sink. The counter was hot against her back from the dishwasher chugging away on lunch and dinner dishes.

Gareth winced. "I don't know how well that'd go over... from either side. I didn't think they'd be gone this long."

"It's not like we have any frame of reference and it's only been, what... four hours?"

"I guess. Watching *Easter Parade* was inspired though, I'll give you that. Who knew your Mom was such a musical nut?"

July laughed. "Everyone who grew up with her as their mom. Dad was... less excited, but at least he understood the goal. Maybe we should look for another movie?"

The garage door smacked against the wall as Toby pushed it open. June followed, holding a baby carrier in both hands. Both of them were grinning and glowing as if they'd been bathing in sun tan oil.

"Where are Mom and Dad?" June set the infant car carrier on the floor as if it contained fine china.

"In the living room flipping stations." July crossed the room and squatted by the baby. A small, slightly conical, head poked out through a nest of pink. Her eyes were shut, lips pursed and wiggling slightly. It was as if a carving knife sliced through July. She frantically built a wall around her heart and took several mental steps backward. "She's cute."

Toby nodded. "Isn't she? You should see her fingers. I've never seen such long, tiny appendages before."

One of the baby's eyes cracked open. The iris rolled around before the lid snapped shut again. June glanced at the clock across the room. "She'll be waking up to eat soon. Let's get her out of the carrier and go show Mom and Dad our baby girl."

July stood and shuffled back a few steps to give a wide berth. Gareth wrapped his arms around her waist and dropped his chin on her shoulder. What was he thinking? Her own thoughts tumbled in her brain.

June cooed as she undid straps and buckles and lifted the infant from the car seat. She turned to look at July. "Want to hold her?"

July's chest constricted. She struggled to breathe as tremors tore through her. Forcing a deep breath into her lungs she shook her head. "That's okay."

June frowned and opened her mouth but Gareth piped up, "If she doesn't, I do."

June placed the baby in Gareth's arms. Everything about him seemed to shine as he drew the child to his chest. "She's so light."

"Let's go see Mom and Dad, they've got to be going nuts. I'm actually surprised they haven't come in here—surely they've heard enough to know we're home." June gripped the carrier and nodded toward the living room.

July trailed behind everyone, bringing up the rear of the procession Gareth led, his cheek resting on the top of the baby's head as he walked. He looked so right holding a baby. She fought the tears that stung her eyes. She should have been able to give him that.

Mom leapt to her feet and squealed, her arms stretching out, fingers wiggling. "Give me that precious child." She grinned as Gareth transferred the baby to her arms. "What's her name?"

June set down the baby carrier and perched on the edge of the coffee table. "Naomi Ashlyn, it means beautiful dream."

17

Betty frowned and turned to June. "What kind of name is that?"

June bit back a sigh and glanced at Toby. She'd told him Mom was going to flip out about the name. He'd said she was overreacting.

"It's a wonderful name." Ed peered over Betty's arm to smile at his granddaughter. "And it has a lovely meaning as well."

The knot in June's belly loosened. "Thanks, Dad. Ashlyn is what her birth mother named her. We wanted to keep that so she'd have something from her biological mom with her all the time. I've always loved the name Naomi and so has Toby."

"But no family names? It's not as if you're going to have tons of opportunities to honor people by naming a child after them. Is it a done deal or do you still have time to change it? I think I remember reading that the birth certificate isn't official until your adoption is finalized. That's not yet, right? Even though you brought her home?"

"Mom." July crossed her arms and shouldered her way into the cluster of people around the baby. "June and Toby can choose whatever name they want. It's *their* child. I'm with Dad, it's lovely."

June shot her sister a grateful smile. Even if July hadn't wanted to hold Naomi, at least she'd stand up for her as needed.

Betty frowned. "Well, I hope you don't end up regretting it."

Naomi's eyes popped open and she let out a wail. June smiled and reached for her. "Here, she's hungry."

"So? Just get me a bottle. It's not like you're breastfeeding." Betty waved a dismissive hand.

June looked at Toby. Now what? Everything they'd read on the subject of bonding said that only the adoptive parents should feed the baby for the first six months or so. And even if they were going to let other people feed her eventually, this was only the second bottle they'd had a chance to give her. Couldn't she be only theirs for the first day?

Toby opened his mouth to speak.

Ed interrupted. "Betty, stop. Give June back her baby. You'll get a chance to dote on her plenty, but she's only a day old and she's only been June and Toby's for a few hours. Let them enjoy it."

Deep lines creased Betty's face as she frowned and, with ill grace, allowed June to scoop Naomi out of her arms. June settled in a chair, murmuring to Naomi, as Toby screwed a nipple onto a pre-mixed bottle of formula and shook it before handing it to June.

"You're not going to waste money on pre-made bottles are you?" Betty scowled at June, reaching over to raise her elbow some and adjust the baby's position.

Toby chuckled. "Nope. I'll head out to the store in a bit and get the essentials. We only ran in for a car seat on our way to the hospital. They sent us home with these, thankfully. We figured you'd want to see everyone as soon as possible, so we skipped the shopping on the way back to the house."

June set the bottle aside and moved Naomi to her shoulder. She began to pat the baby's back. Why had she thought her mother would manage to simply be happy for them? Of course she was going to correct or complain about every little thing. And they'd been home what, twenty minutes? How were they supposed to get any time with the baby if Mom and Dad were staying with them? She shot July a look, pleading for help.

July cleared her throat. "Mom, Dad, why don't you come stay with us for the rest of your visit? I don't imagine you want to be waking up all night long with a newborn."

"Nonsense." Betty shook her head. "June will need our help. In fact, Ed, maybe we should think about staying for a week or so instead of heading back on Tuesday morning."

A week or more? June would lose her mind. Toby would lose his mind, and he was usually unflappable. "Mom. We're just not set up for that right now..."

"Please. We're fine in your guest room, even if it is minuscule. And believe me, you'll be desperate for help after a few nights with a newborn. Besides, this is my granddaughter. You wouldn't deny me the chance to get to know her, would you?" Betty held out her arms for the baby.

June sighed and resumed feeding Naomi. She fought a smile at her mother's annoyed huff.

"Betty, hon, we can't change our plans at this point. I've already rescheduled Niagara once and I'm not sure Charlie and May will be able to meet us there if we change it again. Plus, don't you remember how much you hated having your mother around after the girls were born? She drove you crazy. With the best of intentions, surely, but you couldn't get rid of her fast enough. New moms need their space. We'll plan to come back over the summer, once everyone's settled a bit." Ed pushed himself out of the couch. "Now, I think I'll go ahead on upstairs and read in bed for a bit, but I'm calling dibs on holding Naomi first thing tomorrow. Gotta soak up some baby smell before we leave."

"Night, Dad." June slipped her finger into Naomi's curled fist. The little fingers tightened around hers and June's breath caught. Faith had cautioned them that the birth mother could still change her mind, but they'd cross that bridge if they had to. There was no way she could stop falling in love with this precious bundle simply because she might get ripped out of their life.

Gareth cleared his throat. "I think that's our cue as well. Congrats, guys."

"Yeah. And dinner was great, by the way. I packed the leftovers up in the fridge—want me to fix you a plate before we go?" July glanced between Toby and June.

"Nah, I'll get us something in a bit." Toby clapped Gareth on the shoulder. "Thanks for holding down the fort."

JUNE TIPTOED over to the bassinet and peeked in. Naomi was swaddled snugly in one of the wraps her mother-in-law had sent home with them at Thanksgiving. She looked peaceful. The gentle rise and fall of her chest was mesmerizing. June smiled.

"It's hard to believe she's ours." Toby's whisper in her ear gave her a jolt.

She nodded and eased back, settling on the bed. "It's harder to believe Dad talked Mom into leaving on schedule. Though they don't get to see Charlie and May very often, so maybe that pushed them over the edge."

"Who are they again?" Toby stretched out beside her, pillowing his head on his arm.

"May was Mom's best friend in high school. They roomed

together in college and have been close forever, minus a few tiffs here and there. Fewer than you'd expect, honestly, given my mom. Her husband, Charlie, teaches at a college in upstate New York, so they don't see one another all that often."

"Well, they're in my top ten favorite people now. Make sure we send them a Christmas card." He rolled to his side. "We should probably get some sleep. Who knows when Naomi's going to wake up and need us."

"I guess... it's so nice to watch her sleep though." June slid under the covers and switched off her side-table lamp. "Can you believe she's ours?"

"I'm still holding my breath. Eight more days. I'll believe it in eight days." Toby turned out his light and draped an arm over June, pulling her close.

She snuggled into him, but her brain wouldn't turn off. The birthmother hadn't been a young girl, someone unable to raise a child. No, this woman was older than June, in the middle of a messy divorce, and the child wasn't her husband's. She hadn't even been willing to share her first name with them. Would it hurt Naomi to never know her birthmother's name? Was there some way to protect her from that added pain? Maybe they could get some information, scrubbed of names if that's what the birthmother preferred, from the agency. It'd be good to have at least a modicum of medical data. Either way, given the circumstances of Naomi's birth, it wasn't likely the woman would change her mind in the ten-day post-birth waiting period Virginia required. Even Faith had felt secure enough in the placement that she hadn't pushed them to use the agency's foster care until the papers were signed.

Naomi's soft, snuffling breaths filled the room. June closed her eyes and breathed a heart-felt prayer.

Thank you, Jesus, for this child. Help me to be the best mother I can be. Help me to raise her to love You. Call to her at an early age and draw her near so she doesn't stray from Your side, but lives for

You her whole life. Jesus, let her always know how loved and wanted she is, and never hurt because of the circumstances of her birth. Be with her birthmother, give her peace, draw her to You and bring people into her life who will stand with her through the challenging days ahead.

18

Gareth watched July out of the side of his eye as he drove. "Wanna talk about it?"

She ran a hand through her hair. "Not really. I mean... I dunno."

He snickered. "That clears it up. What's going on, babe?"

"I guess I'm just... struggling. I didn't think it'd be hard, but it is. I'm happy for them. I am. But all I can think of are the babies we lost." She turned and stared out the window. "That's stupid, isn't it?"

He frowned. Stupid wasn't the word he'd choose. Maybe selfish? Better not to suggest that as an alternative. "It's not stupid. Under the circumstances, maybe it's exactly how you should be feeling. I don't know."

"Are you conflicted too?" Hope echoed in her tone.

He wasn't. Not really. Not about this, at least. Bothered by her reaction? Absolutely. Why hadn't she wanted to hold her niece? Okay, sure, she was upset and still hurting from their losses, but here was a new life... couldn't she set that aside and see the possibilities? "Maybe not the same way as you."

"What do you mean?"

He bit back a groan. Why couldn't he keep his trap shut? "I guess I was thinking holding your niece would help you some. Maybe ease some of the ache. You didn't even try though. And I think it hurt June's feelings."

The silence in the car was heavy. Suffocating. Had he said too much? Probably. It was getting harder to keep quiet though. The fiasco with Holly... and now with her texting him all the time... he never got the chance to put it out of his mind, even for a minute. There was always the possibility she'd text again, and that brought the support group and discussion board to mind and before he knew it, he was seething again. Maybe Toby was right. Maybe he needed to talk to someone. It just wasn't going to be July.

"You're right. I should have held her. I just... it doesn't matter. I'll apologize. Try harder next time. This isn't how I pictured today would go though, you know?"

"Sure. If you're like me, you expected barely veiled insults from your mother, strained conversation as your dad tried to smooth things over, either you or June ending up in tears, all ruining an otherwise lovely meal."

A tiny laugh spurted out of July. "Put that way... this was definitely an improvement." She reached over and squeezed his leg. "I'm sorry. I guess I understand how June felt last fall a little better now. I owe her an apology for that, too."

That was a start, at least. Maybe she'd come around—or at least be open to a conversation—if she was starting to realize that her response wasn't the only valid one. Even still, he wasn't ready to attack their issues tonight. But... maybe he'd pray about talking to the pastor.

GARETH SLIPPED from between the covers. He winced as his feet hit the cold floor. Maybe he'd been too hasty to turn off the heat when they got to April—it still got cool enough at night that it was just this side of unpleasant. July's rhythmic breathing filled the room. At least she hadn't had any trouble falling asleep.

He padded downstairs and into the office. Bumping the mouse to wake his computer, he dropped into his desk chair. July's smiling face filled his monitor. His lips curved. It'd been too long since he'd seen that carefree smile in reality. How much of that was his fault?

He blew out a breath and opened a web browser. It wasn't as if he was smiling with carefree abandon much either. And now, having held his niece... whatever progress he'd been making numbing himself to the ache had flown out the window. Why couldn't July understand? Was it because it's supposed to be women who long for children and men don't care either way?

His cell buzzed with an incoming text. His heart plummeted into his stomach. What was it going to take to get Holly to take a hint? Was he going to have to pay for his stupidity forever? It wasn't as if he'd done anything wrong. He hadn't. And yet... if that was the case, why wasn't he telling July about it? Gareth's fingers flew over the keyboard, typing in his search. A few clicks later, he was poking through the settings on his phone. There it was... call block. The website suggested it would work for texts—anything from that number. He punched save and let out a breath. One problem solved. Hopefully.

Gareth leaned back in his chair. His fingers itched to browse to the one forum that still seemed safe from Holly. He'd been more guarded there... but surely they'd understand what holding Naomi had done to him. No. If the issue with Holly had proven anything, it was that just because a discussion group felt anonymous and safe, that didn't mean it was. Who knew if the people on the other end of the screen had even actually gone through any of the stuff they said they had? It wasn't as if the forum required any amount of proof. Heck, you didn't even have to use your real name. Maybe they were all psychos out to prey on people who were hurting.

He'd be better off talking to the Pastor. Heaving a sigh, he clicked on his email program, opened a new message, and began to type.

19

J uly cringed at the pile of folders stacked on her desk. Tax season was officially in full swing. It had been getting worse over the last month but now, with a late Easter finished, she had nine days to power through as much of this as she could. The pile looked larger than it had on Friday.

"Knock knock." Zach, an accountant from the down the hall, poked his head in her office.

"What's up?"

"Did you hear?"

July shook her head. This wouldn't be good. Zach thrived on gossip, but usually left her alone since she made it clear she wasn't going to actively participate. For him to seek her out anyway... her stomach sank and she eyed the files. They must be divvying up someone's work.

"Geoff was unceremoniously escorted out on Friday night, late. Apparently, he got caught helping one of his larger clients with two sets of books. I'm guessing you'll get the majority of his individual clients."

"I think I already have them. I was wondering why my stack

looked bigger. But this can't be all of them—it's not much taller than it was when I left for the weekend."

Zach's grin had a mercenary gleam. "They're packing his office right now. Whatever's been added to that stack there is just the tip of the iceberg. Happy tax season."

She waited until he pushed himself off her doorway and sauntered out of sight before lowering her head into her hands. So much for having a chance to see Gareth for the next nine days. Not that she'd planned to be able to see a ton of him, but she usually managed to get home for a late dinner and skip working on Sunday. Not this year.

July pushed to her feet and trudged down the hall to Geoff's old office. Tina, her boss' secretary, stood in the corner with a clipboard. Lisa, the firm's receptionist, called out client names as she tucked them into file boxes.

"Good morning, ladies."

Tina rolled her eyes. "It's not a good morning and, given that Zach was just in here digging for the scoop, you probably already know that."

"I tried." July nodded toward the stack of file boxes. "How many of those am I ending up with?"

Lisa sat back on her heels and dragged her arm across her forehead. "Just two of them. The big stack in the corner is all archival. Why he didn't trust our backup system is beyond me."

July's gaze slid to Tina who gave a minute shake of her head. If he'd been helping cook the books for clients over the years, he'd need his own backups. More than likely, if a need arose for the corporate backups, the files were mysteriously missing or damaged and Geoff came across as a superhero for having been a packrat. But apparently Lisa didn't know about the reasons for his dismissal. July gave it 'til lunch before she heard. Zach had his teeth sunk deep in the scandalous affair and he'd make sure everyone with ears heard about it.

"You never know with some people. But that'll be a project

for me, most likely. Sorting through to determine what we need to save and what can be destroyed. At least that can wait until after the fifteenth." Tina made a few more marks on her clipboard. "That finishes off my list. Any more files, Lisa?"

Lisa shook her head, dropped a lid on the box, and pushed to her feet. "All yours, July. Need a hand?"

"If you don't mind grabbing one, I can take the other. Or I can make two trips if you need to get out front." July hefted one of the boxes.

"You're on the way. That's all you needed me for, right, Tina?" Lisa groaned as she picked up the file box.

"For now. I might grab you again later. My biggest priority was transferring the clients that still need their taxes filed. Thanks for the help."

Who was going to audit all the records that had already been filed? July shook her head as she made her way back to her office, Lisa shuffling behind her. Probably everyone. The usual lull that came after tax season didn't appear to be in the cards this year. Wouldn't that just make everyone's day?

"I DIDN'T THINK you'd be at work today." July unwrapped the candy bar she'd snagged from the vending machine on the ground floor of her office building. The cherry blossoms continued to hang on, despite attempts of the spring breeze to dislodge them from their branches. Still, it wouldn't be long before the ground was covered in a snow-fall of petals.

June huffed. "I hadn't planned to be. I called Bob this morning, intending to go on maternity leave, effective immediately, but apparently there was a problem with the delivery we made on Friday so I needed to come in and get it straightened out first."

"Why couldn't he fix it? Or your team?" July resisted the

urge to glance at the time. She shouldn't be taking this break... though maybe it would help clear her head and let her focus better for the rest of the afternoon. Weren't you supposed to get up and move every so often for increased productivity?

"Ha. My team is next to useless. Henry's out again with some babysitter issue. Phong is on a vacation he's had scheduled for three weeks, and Jill...is good at what she does, but her strong suit isn't really in the high-pressure environment."

July chuckled and crumpled the wrapper into a ball, the last bit of candy lodging in a sticky lump in her throat. She cleared her throat and swallowed, working her tongue side to side to get it to go down. "Listen to you. That's management potential right there."

"Har-de-har. Although..." June's eyes narrowed as she looked at July. "Do you think I'm stupid for wanting to stay home with Naomi?"

July's eyes lifted. This was the first she'd heard of that notion. Though it wasn't something they'd discussed in great length in a while. When you get caught up trying to have a baby, what happens next seems to fall by the wayside. "Not if that's what you and Toby think is best, no. Why?"

"Mom."

"Ah. It's the second verse of the 'I didn't pay for you to go to college to get married the minute you graduate' speech, isn't it?" July rubbed the back of her neck. What was wrong with her mother that she couldn't simply be happy for her daughters?

"Basically. I've worked so hard to get where I am, it's expensive to live in this area, you'll lose who you are and resent Toby and Naomi. Blah, blah, blah. I don't understand it, really. She stayed home with us until we were in school. Did she hate it that much?"

"I don't think she hated it. I'm not sure she would've been happy no matter what she chose." July glanced down at her cell phone and winced. "I have to get back to work. I just got two boxes of clients dropped on my desk and I was already pushing my nine days to the limit. Now... I'll probably be spending three of those days filing extensions for anyone whose taxes are going to take more than a couple of hours. And that's unlikely to go over well with the clients or my boss."

"Ugh. Forgot it was tax season. I'll let you run. Just thought I'd swing by, since I'm here, and, well... this might be our last lunch in the courtyard. If I don't come back from maternity leave..."

July's stomach sank. How could things change so quickly? Why did they have to? It didn't matter. Right now wasn't the time to deal with it. She forced a smile. "I'm sure that's not true. You'll want to get of the house sometime, right? So you and Naomi can come up and we'll sit on our bench together."

June brightened. "That's a great idea. But not during tax season. Go. I know you've got a ton to do and I don't want to be the reason you don't see Gareth tonight."

20

A fter July disappeared around a corner, June sighed. She might bring Naomi to visit July for lunch, but it wouldn't be the same. Already it was as if July was pulling away. Why hadn't she wanted to hold the baby? She hadn't asked about Naomi at all. No, 'how was the first night at home?' or 'Did you get any sleep?' None of that. If the shoe was on the other foot, June would've been asking about the baby non-stop.

June stood and headed back toward her office. She had most of the problem resolved and Bob was content to stand in for her until next week when Phong was back. He could handle the team during her maternity leave. Would he be her replacement? Did she really want to stay home? Was her mother right and she'd be bored and frustrated within a month? Maybe that's why they gave you six weeks of maternity leave. Maybe it was just long enough for you to realize that you didn't want to quit your job after all. But in six weeks they'd be coming up on another deadline. How miserable was it going to be coming back to work in the middle of what was inevitably going to be a nightmare?

Waiting for the light to cross the street, she called home.

"Hey, babe. You on your way home?"

"Maybe another hour, tops. I think I've got everything straight here. How's Naomi doing?"

"She's great, isn't she?" Toby's voice went up into his charming baby voice. "We're hanging out with Daddy and Grandma and Grandpa and no one has killed anyone yet. Isn't that right?"

June laughed. "I take it Mom's fighting you tooth and nail to have all the baby time?"

"Something like that." His voice returned to normal. "Though your Dad's been surprisingly helpful in keeping her in check. There might be hope for her yet."

"Nah. It'll be short-lived at best, and someone will end up paying. Probably Dad. Nice of him to take one for the team. Did you remember to call your folks?"

"Yeah. They're going to try to come the first week of July, spend a week, if that's okay? They didn't want to crowd us right away and figured we might need a month to settle in."

"I love your mother. That sounds perfect. I'm not sure where they'll sleep..." June darted across the road as soon as the 'walk' sign lit up. They never gave you enough time to get all the way from one side to the other unless you ran. "The crib isn't going to fit in the room with the current guest bed."

"I was actually talking to your dad about that this morning. He had the idea to get a daybed with a pop up trundle. Then it's like having two twins or you can push them together into a King—though I'm not sure that would actually work once all of Naomi's stuff is in there. But the two twins might work if we put one on each wall. I thought maybe we could poke around online when you get back and see what our options are." A wail filled her ear. "Ooh, gotta run. Someone's hungry. Love you, see you soon."

The line went dead. June smiled and slid her phone back

into her pocket. How someone so teensy could make such a noise was... fascinating. She'd go with fascinating. At two in the morning, her word choices had been less reserved. But they'd get the hang of it. All the books said you hit a routine within a week or so.

JUNE DROPPED her things inside the door, toed off her shoes, and poked her head into the living room. Toby slouched on the sofa, his feet on the coffee table. Naomi was nestled on his shoulder. Both were asleep. June's heart melted. She tiptoed back into the kitchen and dug her phone out of her purse. She needed a photo. Toby might object to having a snapshot of him sleeping, but it was too precious to resist. Finished, she headed upstairs. Mom and Dad must be napping too. The door to their room was shut. She leaned close. Soft snores drifted through the door and sparked a jaw-cracking yawn. If everyone else was napping, maybe she ought to as well.

She changed out of her work clothes into pajamas. It didn't matter that it was barely three in the afternoon. If she was napping, she was going to be comfortable. Besides, they weren't taking Naomi out anywhere for the first week, so she had no plans to leave the house.

Mom would comment.

June hesitated. Did it matter what her mother thought? She was a mother herself, now. Didn't that change the relationship somehow? Shouldn't it? Knowing her mother, probably not. If being married and out of the house hadn't done it, why would having her own daughter? She wasn't going to be like that. Naomi, and any other children they might have, needed to be free to have their own opinions. She and Toby would do the best they could in the time they had them, but when they were grown they'd just be friends.

"It's not that easy, you know."

June's hand flew to her mouth as she turned. Had she been talking out loud? Heat flooded her face. "Mom..."

"I heard you tiptoe by, thought I'd come see how work was." Betty perched on the edge of the bed. "You were muttering to yourself. I shouldn't have listened... but I'm glad I did. I guess I owe you an apology."

"No. Mom..."

Betty patted the bed. "Come and sit. You're not completely wrong. I have had trouble letting you and your sister grow up. You've both always been so self-sufficient. Even as children, I never felt like you needed me because you had each other. And after all that your father and I went through to have you... I didn't handle it well."

June drew her eyebrows together. "What do you mean, 'all your father and I went through'?"

Betty heaved a sigh. "It's something I should have told both of you a long time ago, but it never seemed to come up. And then, last year when you and July both did all those procedures, I couldn't. I tried. Your father told me I needed to. But I couldn't. It was such a horrible time in my life and in our marriage... I didn't want to relive it."

"What are you saying?"

"We tried for years to conceive with no luck at all. So we finally scraped together everything we could afford and found a specialist. It wasn't like it is today. You didn't talk about doing IVF. It was risky and controversial and not many people did it. Didn't you ever wonder why there weren't any other twins in the family?"

June shrugged. The thought had occurred once or twice, but it wasn't as if having twins was a commonplace occurrence, even in families when it was more likely. "I still... I... why weren't you more supportive when we decided on that route if you'd been through it?"

Tears brimmed in Betty's eyes and she looked away. "I don't know. Maybe I felt guilty? After all, you have my faulty genes... I'm sorry."

Still grappling with the implications of her mother's words, June opened her mouth then snapped it shut. Restless cries echoed up the stairwell. In spite of herself, June smiled. "Sounds like everyone's done napping. Let's go downstairs. I want to hold my baby girl."

21

Gareth shut off the engine and dropped his head back. This was entirely too familiar. Was there even any point to being here? After all, Pastor Brown was just going to tell him he needed to talk to July. The one thing he didn't see any point in trying to do. Beyond that, what could the pastor possibly have to offer?

A tap at the passenger window made him jump.

"You coming in, or did you want to meet in your car?" A smile ghosted around the corner of Paul's mouth. "It's more comfy in my office, and Mary made an apple cake this afternoon. I'm pretty sure we can sweet talk her out of some."

With a short laugh, Gareth pushed open the car door. "You pushed me over the edge with the apple cake. That's an offer that's hard to refuse."

He followed the pastor into the house and took a seat in the study while Paul continued down the hallway that led to the kitchen. Gareth's stomach grumbled. With July in her tax season crazy hours, he hadn't bothered with dinner at home. He'd planned to drive through somewhere when he got hungry enough to care. Or forage in the fridge. But apple cake had fruit in it, so it had to be sort of healthy. It'd do. And there were several burger joints on the way home if it didn't.

"Here we are. I had her go ahead and plop some ice cream on top of it. Hope that's okay?" Paul grinned and offered Gareth a dish.

Gareth eyed the generous portion. He wouldn't be needing a hamburger, that was for sure. "Ice cream is always a winner."

"So. What brings you here, Gareth? You didn't say much in your email." Concern flickered across Paul's features.

Gareth poked at the ice cream and cake in his dish, scooping a bite onto the spoon then dropping it back into the bowl. "You remember when we were here in the fall? Of course you do. Well, the deal we made was that we'd try IVF and then, if it didn't work out, we'd look into adoption. That way, July got to try what her heart was set on, even though it wasn't something I was really excited about and, if it failed, we'd look into where my heart was leading."

Paul nodded and took a bite of dessert.

"Well now July's completely set against adoption. She won't even go to an information meeting. She just wants to be done and close the book on children." Gareth looked down at the ice cream melting in his bowl and set the dish aside. "I'm... struggling to accept that."

"Hmm. I can see how you would be. What did July say?"

"I haven't told her. I agreed to go along with it because I can't face the possibility of another fight like we had in the fall. It took so long to get back from that... how can I willingly go back there?"

Paul arched a brow but said nothing.

Gareth picked up his dessert and began smushing the ice cream into the cake, blending the textures into a soupy concoction. He spooned a bite. The cold, crumb-filled stew sliding down his throat did nothing to ease the heat coursing through his body. He clenched his jaw, his teeth grinding together.

"So what have you been doing about your anger?" Paul shifted and set his empty bowl on the desk behind him.

"Ignoring it, mostly. Or trying to. I spent some time online —there are these discussion groups, support group type things. But that didn't work out so well. So now... I don't know what to do."

"Tell me about the online groups. That sounds like it might be positive—a place to talk to other Christian men who are sharing a similar struggle?"

Gareth shook his head. Why hadn't he thought to look for a Christian support group? Or at least limit his search to groups for men? How, in one sentence, had the pastor managed to clarify exactly how stupid Gareth was without saying those words? He cleared his throat. "Yeah, well... it wasn't just Christian men. In fact, it was primarily women—or at least people who said they were women. I've discovered that the Internet community isn't always truthful."

Paul offered a tiny smile. "What happened?"

The story of meeting with Holly spilled out. "At the end of the night, I realized that I was lucky Toby came with me. It could have gotten ugly. I would never cheat on July, that's simply not something I'm willing to consider. But that woman could easily have made it look like I had. And who knows what she'd have done then?"

"I'm grateful a close call was all it took to bring you around. Do you have any idea the number of people I, or someone at the church, counsel on a weekly basis for addictions and infidelities that all started innocently enough on the Internet? And then, before they realized what was happening, they were embroiled in a full-blown emotional—or sometimes even physical—affair. All because of a post here or a click there."

Gareth stared down at his shoes. Had he been on his way toward that? Even with his assurances that he wouldn't cheat on July, hadn't he done so, sort of, by sharing his thoughts with Holly instead of Jules?

"You've gotten offline then?" Paul crossed his legs.

Gareth nodded. "I emailed you instead."

"Definitely a better choice. The Internet can't give you apple cake. Or creamy apple sauce, which is what it looks like yours has become."

"Sorry. It's still delicious." Gareth spooned another bite, catching a dribble with his tongue before it dripped down his chin.

"If you don't want to talk to July about it right now—I say right now because, ultimately, you're going to have to have a conversation with her if things are going to be right between the two of you—what do you want from me? What do you think I can do to help?"

He was the pastor. Wasn't he supposed to have the answers? Why did he always only have questions? Gareth's shoulders fell. "I don't know. I was hoping you'd have some ideas."

"It turns out, I have a couple. But I wanted to see if you had something in mind first. However, since you're looking for my advice, let's start with your anger—you agree that you're angry?"

Gareth nodded.

"Then let's start there because anger, left unchecked and unresolved, turns into bitterness. And that doesn't help anyone. Do you know the story behind Kevin and Lydia's marriage?"

Where was this going? He searched his memory—surely July had mentioned something about it at some point. "Vaguely."

"The short version is that Lydia had an abortion and turned to all kinds of terrible things to numb the pain. When Kevin found out about it, it nearly broke him. He was angry—justifiably so. Around that same time, God put him in a place where he witnessed some of the work that Pregnancy Resource

Centers do with women who have had an abortion. One of the things they do is help the women—and men—identify the roots of their anger."

The roots? It wasn't complicated—July had gone back on her word. "I'm not sure how that would help. I know why I'm angry."

Paul gave a slow nod. "You probably think you do. And some of it is probably true. But there are more than likely some layers in there that you haven't thought about. Until you uncover all of them and face them head on, you can't get rid of the anger."

"Okay... how do I do that?" It was worth a try, though it was unlikely there'd be anything more than July going back on her word. She promised, then changed her mind and expected him to fall in line. Honestly, wasn't that reason enough to be upset?

"When you get home, take a piece of paper and draw a few flowers near the top half."

"Flowers? I'm not really an artist..."

"They don't have to be beautiful. Try a dandelion. Big puffy ball, long stem. Done. And that's a bonus reminder because they're weeds, just like anger. Something we want to get rid of. Then, draw lines coming off the stems—the roots. And label the roots. Put down everyone and everything about this situation that makes you mad."

"I'm only going to need one root." Gareth crossed his arms.

Paul pursed his lips and was silent for several heartbeats. "That may be the case, but humor me."

"All right. Then what?"

"Then you bring it with you on Thursday night and we'll talk about it."

"Thursday?"

"Are you free?"

July was going to be working long hours. There was nothing waiting for him at home and there never would be. "Sure."

"Great." Paul grinned. "Can I pray for you before you go?"

Gareth nodded.

"Heavenly Father, we come to you tonight with heavy hearts. There's much about this situation that only You know. But what I know is that Gareth is hurting and angry and he needs to feel Your presence with him. Help him to see all the roots of his anger—past his feelings of betrayal to anything else that's factoring into his desire to hide his hurt from his wife. Reveal Your love to him. In Jesus' name, amen."

"Amen." Betrayal. Gareth hadn't put that label on July's actions, but it fit. Something in his chest loosened. "Thanks."

"Anytime. Now," Paul nodded to the soup in Gareth's bowl, "why don't you bring that back to the kitchen and I'll have Mary get you a new dish. Maybe some coffee?"

Gareth stood. "No, that's okay. But thanks. I... I think I'm going to swing by and see my new niece before heading home."

Paul stood and offered his hand. "I heard about that. Pass on our congratulations, would you? We're praying everything goes smoothly for them as well. See you Thursday?"

"Yeah. Thursday."

The pastor stood in the door until Gareth pulled away from the curb. He gave a little wave before heading back toward the highway. Should he call first? It was only seven thirty. June and Toby should still be up. What about Naomi? Did infants have a bedtime? No idea. But even if she was asleep, maybe they'd let him peek in at her.

He grabbed his cell phone and dialed July.

"Hey, sweetie. I was just thinking about you."

He grinned. "Really? Good thoughts, I hope."

"Always." She paused. "You're on your cell—what are you out doing?"

"Thought I'd go see the baby and your folks. June and Toby too, since they're there. Maybe beg some dinner since my hard-working wife is stuck at the office." No point in mentioning his visit to the pastor yet. It would only raise questions he wasn't ready to answer.

"Give them my love. I saw June at lunch, briefly. She's thinking of staying home. That was never something she'd talked about before. I was surprised."

"If they can afford it, it's great. Around here it's hard though. You'll still see plenty of her, Jules, if that's what's bothering you." Gareth flicked on his turn signal and changed lanes.

July sighed. "I guess that's it. I don't know."

"How are the taxes going? Making progress?"

She groaned. "Some. I managed to separate the stacks into those that I think I can actually get filed in time and those that I'm going to have to file an extension for. I'm trying to get all the extension paperwork taken care of tonight so I can move those out of my immediate brain space and focus."

"You can do it. I have faith in you."

"Aww. Thanks, Gar. That means a lot. Drive safe."

"Will do. I love you."

"Love you too."

He dropped his phone into the cup holder and drummed his fingers on the steering wheel. Why did June's desire to stay home surprise July? Hadn't she wanted to stay home with their kids? He'd always assumed she would. Was it just an assumption? Surely they'd talked about it and were on the same page... just like they'd been on the same page about adoption. He blew out a breath. Did he know his wife at all anymore?

"Where's my niece?" Gareth stretched out his arms as Toby opened the door.

"And hello to you, too." Toby chuckled. "She's in with the grandparents. Good luck prying her out of their grasp."

Gareth rubbed his hands together. "I have my ways."

He followed Toby into the living room of the town house. June peered over Betty's shoulder as the older woman tickled the baby's chin. Ed beamed at them from his chair.

"Gareth." Ed's voice boomed, startling a cry from Naomi. "What brings you all this way?"

"I came to see the two of you off. I know you're leaving in the morning and I didn't want to miss my chance to say good-bye." He settled on the couch next to Betty. "Have you had a good trip, Mom?"

She shook her head at him. "Don't think I don't see what you're doing, young man. You came to see us off? Please. It's this little darling right here who brought you to the Virginia side of the river, and no one else. But, since you took the time to be creative I'll let you hold her."

Gareth grinned and gathered Naomi into his arms, leaning in to nuzzle his nose to hers. "There's my girl. Have they started spoiling you rotten yet? 'Cause it's coming, I just know it."

"Is not." June flicked his shoulder. "She's going to be a perfectly well-behaved little girl."

"With every imaginable privilege," Ed whispered.

"I heard that, Dad." June frowned.

Toby laughed. "You should see yourself June. Of course she's going to be spoiled. But within moderation."

"Spoiled in moderation." Gareth's shook his head. "That's a good one."

"So really, what brings you out this way? It's a week night. And why isn't July...a-ha. I know why you're here. You're hungry." June stood and started toward the kitchen. "I'll go fix you a plate."

Toby shot Gareth a quizzical look.

"Tax season's in full swing. Frankly, I'm surprised she hasn't been pulling crazy hours before now, but she got a slew of new files dumped on her today so it's going to be even worse than usual this year." Gareth gave Naomi a gentle jiggle. "When will she smile?"

"It'll be a bit, yet. I think the books say two or three months. She'll get there. For now, you can enjoy her Winston Churchill impression."

"Toby." Betty frowned. "That's absolutely no way to speak about your daughter. She's beautiful."

"He was joking, Betty. Give the boy a break. Now, Gareth, you just pass that bundle of sweetness over here and you dig into the plate June's brought. One of the gals from your Sunday school class stopped by with it earlier this evening and it's mighty tasty."

"Who?" Gareth transferred Naomi and reached for the plate June offered. "Smells good."

"Laura brought it by. She said when she was a new mom, meals were the only help she ever needed. She even brought a different dish already frozen to put away for a tough day." June shrugged. "I'm not sure I really get the bringing meals thing, but I didn't give birth, either. Maybe that makes a difference?"

"Don't look at me. I'm a guy. I like to eat. I don't really care where the food comes from."

Toby chuckled. "That was, essentially, my response. I'm not turning down free food. Just because I can cook—or order in— doesn't mean I always want to."

"Will you try and drive all the way to Niagara tomorrow, Dad, or are you stopping half-way?" Gareth dipped his fork back into the cheesy casserole. It was sort of like mac and cheese, but there were too many other things in there for such a mundane label. He'd have to try to weasel the recipe out of Laura on Sunday.

"I want to stop and see Gettysburg on our way up. It'll be about time for a break then anyway, knowing Betty's bladder and tolerance for sitting long periods in the car. But more than likely that'll mean we spend the night somewhere in Northern Pennsylvania before finishing up the trek to Niagara. We're not due there until Wednesday anyway. So we've got the time." Ed kissed Naomi's head. "Betty's trying to convince me to stay an extra day here and drive straight, but I don't see that working. It's a good eight hours from here. If we're going to keep our dinner reservation on Wednesday night, we need to make it a two-day trip."

Betty grunted. "It's ridiculous to worry about a dinner reservation when we have a granddaughter to see now."

Gareth scraped the plate and set it aside. There was no point in stepping into that argument. Betty'd be upset if they missed dinner with their friends, too. She'd get over it once they were on their way. How Ed put up with that woman was anyone's guess, but they'd managed to raise two incredible women, so something they were doing had to be working. "Let me have my niece back for a minute and then I'll get out of your hair. I want to take a nap before July gets home."

"When will she leave work?" Betty's eyes followed Naomi as she was shifted between the men.

"In the past it's been around midnight. But with the co-worker's load that got dropped on her today, it'll probably be later than that."

"Don't let her work herself too hard." June leaned over and adjusted the blanket wrapped around the baby.

Gareth scoffed. "I'll do what I can. Still, it's the accountant's life. Most of the year is pretty tolerable, but tax season is a bear. Secretly, I think she thrives on the chaos since she knows it has a finite, predictable end."

"That sounds like July. She was always one who could handle high stress as long as it didn't go on for too long. June, on the other hand, was always a planner who'd do anything to avoid the stress in the first place." Betty shook her head. "It boggles the mind how twins can be so different."

"We're fraternal twins, Mom. It's not as if we look alike." June tucked her hair behind her ears.

"I think that's my cue." Gareth passed Naomi to Betty's waiting arms and stood. "Thanks for dinner and the snuggles. I'll probably swing by again later this week, if that's okay? It's nice to break up the boredom of being home alone all evening."

"Definitely." Toby clapped him on the shoulder and walked with him to the front door. "You okay?"

Gareth peered around his brother-in-law. He nodded. "I was at the Pastor's, so I didn't come all this way just for Naomi."

"Go okay?"

He shrugged. "Lots to think about. We'll see. I wasn't wrong though, his first question was whether or not I'd talked to July about it."

Toby cocked his head to the side. "Any plans to do that?"

"Not yet. But I guess I'm going to have to figure out how to get there."

Toby nodded. "I'll keep praying."

Gareth tucked his hands in his pockets and strode to the car. Part of him wanted to stay, even if meant hearing Betty go on and on about the differences between June and July. Holding that baby left him warm all over, even if it also increased the throbbing pain in his heart. Nah. It was better to go home and get that nap. Then he'd be able to do more than grunt when July told him about her day.

22

J une stopped in the doorway of their second bedroom and put her hands on her hips. Mom and Dad had left after breakfast and, now that Naomi was snuggled in for a nap, it was time to tackle her room.

"Where are we going to put all this stuff?"

Toby edged past her into the room. "No idea. Some of it can stay, but in the long run I'm thinking we'll need to finish the basement. It doesn't make sense to have no guest room. And while the daybed idea is a good one, what happens when Naomi is older and needs that bed for herself?"

"I guess. It's not like we get a ton of visitors. Maybe a pull out sofa for the living room?"

He frowned. "Can you see either of our parents being happy with that? Plus, there's hardly any privacy. At least in the basement they'd have a place to go and get away from the chaos if they wanted."

June nodded. Their town house was homey, but it really was much more suited to a couple with no kids. There were plenty of families in the neighborhood who made it work—it was a worthwhile tradeoff being so close to everything—but did she really want to be one of them? "That's down the road though. And speaking of the basement... is there room to store the bed down there? I think we can leave the dresser, maybe put a changing pad on top of it and have it do double duty. But the crib and the bed aren't both going to fit."

"I can move a few things around. Maybe it's time to admit that a dedicated rec room isn't going to work in this house. She's going to need a place for toys before too long, and the living room might not be the best solution for that."

"Let's worry about one thing at a time. Did you bring the drill up? I'll start disassembling the bed if you go make room for it."

Toby brought the drill in from the hallway and handed it to her before disappearing again. June ran her hand along the smooth cherry bed frame. It had been a wedding gift from his parents. They'd used it for a while, until Toby had realized June was a restless sleeper and a double bed wasn't conducive to either of them actually sleeping. Setting it up in the basement wasn't a terrible idea. There was a rough-in for a bathroom down there and they could wall off a small space for the bed. It wouldn't count as a legal bedroom, but it would work well enough for guests. Having the rest of the area finished would be nice. It was just a matter of time. And money.

Toby came back up just as she was loosening the last bolt on the footboard. He caught it as it started to fall. "I'll take this down and be back up for the mattress and box spring."

"Need help?"

"I think I've got it. I'll holler if that changes."

"Holler quietly. Naomi's still asleep and I'd like it to stay that way a little longer."

He grinned and left the room with the footboard.

Six more days. Naomi wouldn't officially be theirs for six more days. Was it stupid to get the nursery ready before the birthmother signed her paperwork? And why wouldn't she at least let them know her first name? How would she explain that to Naomi down the road? The truth, obviously. But it was going to hurt her... there had to be some way to soften that, didn't there?

With the bed disassembled and relegated to the basement, the nine by nine room seemed much more livable. They were definitely going to have to stick to a twin bed as Naomi got older. Maybe bunk beds. That was a worry for another day, one down the road quite a bit.

"I think the crib is heavier than the double was." Toby pushed the box holding the unassembled crib into the room.

"Sturdy. Let's focus on how nice and sturdy it's going to be." She cocked her head. "Did you hear that?"

He nodded. "Yep. Why don't you go get her, I'll get started on this. I can probably get it together on my own."

With a nod, she crossed into their bedroom. Naomi grunted and squeaked from the bassinet. June's stomach fluttered as she looked down and met Naomi's steady blue gaze. "Hi baby girl. You're awake sooner than I expected."

She lifted her out of the bassinet and held her close, breathing deeply. There was nothing quite like the smell of baby. She sniffed. Especially one who needed a change. "That's okay, Naomi, Mommy still loves you. We'll get that changed then see how Daddy's doing."

June grabbed a diaper from the package next to the bed and tugged the changing pad and wipes box closer. She unsnapped the pink and green striped jammies Mom had rushed out to buy yesterday and wrinkled her nose. How could someone so small make such a big stink? The phone rang.

"Tobe? Can you get that?"

"Kind of in the middle of something."

She looked down at the full diaper and Naomi's arched back and flailing feet. "Yeah, me too."

Rustling and grumbling echoed down the hall before Toby

stomped into the room. "What... oh. You win." He grabbed the phone. "Hello?"

June cleaned the baby's backside and wrangled her into a clean diaper. Why wouldn't she lie still? It would go so much faster. She checked Naomi's umbilical stump and swabbed it with an alcohol wipe. The books all gave different suggestions for its care, but their doctor had said to use alcohol, so that's what she was going with. If no one could agree, it probably wasn't a huge deal either way. It did look like it was starting to dry up. Might be time for a real bath before long.

She glanced up at Toby and froze. "What's going on?"

"Hang on." Toby covered the mouthpiece. "It's Faith. Naomi's birthmother wants to see her. They're going to set up a time at the agency office. We can stay... but she could decide to take Naomi home with her."

June's knees buckled and she sank to the floor. This couldn't be happening. The woman hadn't wanted to see Naomi in the hospital, or meet them. What had changed? It had seemed so certain.

"Okay. Yeah. Two o'clock. We'll... we'll be there." Toby clicked off the phone and crossed to June. He scooped Naomi off the bed and lowered himself to the floor. "It's going to be okay. Faith said this happens. Sometimes they just want to make sure they've done the right thing, that the baby's being well cared for. She said not to worry."

June let out a strangled sob and reached for the baby. She tucked Naomi's feet back into her jammies and redid the snaps before holding her close. A tear slid down her cheek and plopped onto Naomi's head. "I can't..."

"Neither can I." He draped his arm around June's shoulder and pulled her in. "We have to trust that God's going to take care of us."

She took a deep breath. *Oh, God... You know I can't handle losing Naomi. Please... please don't take her away. Please... just don't.*

EYES BURNING WITH UNSHED TEARS, June carried Naomi in her car seat up the steps to the adoption agency. Her fingers tightened around Toby's. "Say it again."

"We'll get through this. It'll be okay."

She swallowed the lump in her throat. They'd be okay. But oh...this baby girl was hers already.

"Hi June. Toby." Faith met them at the end of the hall with a tight but warm smile. "I know this is hard, but I really think she's just looking for reassurance."

June pressed a hand to her chest, but it did nothing to ease the tightness. "We can stay?"

Faith nodded. "Unless she asks you not to. She may want a few minutes alone. Try not to read too much into that. Ready?"

Toby shook his head. "No. But I don't think waiting is going to help. Let's just get this over with."

June clenched the handle of the car seat. Naomi was asleep. She looked so peaceful and perfect. Would her birthmother realize how much they already loved her? Dragging her feet, she followed Faith into the den-like room where they'd had all their meetings at the agency previously.

A woman who looked to be in her late thirties slumped in a chair. She was pale, but neatly put together in clothes from a higher-end catalog that June sometimes ordered from herself.

"Hi." June tried to push her mouth into a smile. Had it looked friendly? She'd been aiming for friendly, but the herd of hula-hooping elephants in her stomach made it hard to focus.

The woman nodded and stretched forward, trying her best to peer into the car seat. "Is that her?"

Toby squeezed June's hand then let it go. He pried the carrier out of June's grasp and turned it so the woman could see. "It is. She's beautiful, isn't she?"

Something flickered in the woman's eyes and she gave a short nod. "She sleeping okay? And eating?"

Snap out of it, June. "Yeah. She's up every two hours, sometimes two and a half, to eat. We've been trying to follow an eat, play, sleep schedule, but it's nothing rigid. She drifted off in the car on the way here."

"Can I... can I hold her?" The woman's gaze flicked between June and Toby. Could she be as nervous as they were?

"Of course." Toby set the carrier on the floor and unbuckled Naomi. He eased her out of the seat and into the woman's arms.

The woman sat stiffly for several heartbeats before she finally drew the baby closer to her chest.

July licked her lips. "Would it be okay if we asked your first name? At the hospital, Faith said you didn't want to exchange any of that information. But... I'd really love to have a name to tell her when we talk about you with her."

From behind the woman, Faith caught June's eye and gave her an encouraging nod. June held her breath as she waited for an answer.

"Betty. My name's Betty."

The ice around June's heart thawed and her stomach settled. That couldn't be a coincidence, could it? "That's my mother's name."

Betty's eyes flicked up. "Really? Her name-name, not a nickname for Elizabeth?"

"Actually, yeah. My grandmother always said there was no point in giving someone a name just to have the rest of the world shorten it later."

Betty smiled. It took ten years off her and left her looking friendly and warm. "That's why I liked Ashlyn, though I guess you could easily call her Ash. Or Lyn. But it doesn't really need shortening. Will you keep it? The name?"

June glanced at Toby. Should they mention adding Naomi

to the front? Would that help or hurt their chances of this ending well?

"We hoped to use it as a middle name. It means dream, did you know that?" Toby perched on the edge of couch, facing Betty. "So we thought Naomi might go nicely in front of it. Then she'd be our beautiful dream come true."

A tear slid down Betty's cheek. "That's perfect."

June scooted over to where Toby sat and lowered herself beside him, her breath catching in her chest. What did that mean? She watched Betty cradle Naomi and forced her hands to stay in her lap instead of reaching out for the baby.

"Will you tell me your names? I'd like to be able to think about her with you and know who I'm thinking of."

Air whooshed out of June's lungs. "I'm June. This is Toby."

Betty kissed Naomi's head and held her out. "Here. You can take her back. Thank you. I just needed to remember why I was doing this. It's better this way. It's right."

June gathered Naomi close and looked at Betty. "Could we have Faith take our picture together? The four of us? I think Naomi would like having that later on."

"Can we get one on my phone, too?"

Faith stepped forward and took both cell phones. "Absolutely. And I'll get another with the agency camera in case any of you want one that's not off a phone. Lean in just a bit, now, and say cheese."

"As soon as she said her name was Betty, I knew we were going to be okay." Toby eased back on the sofa, careful not to jostle Naomi who was asleep on his shoulder.

"You're more optimistic than me. Though I'll admit it helped with some of the paralyzing terror."

He chuckled. "It wasn't that bad."

"Maybe not for you. I honestly wasn't sure if we'd come home with a baby or not. Now I feel like I can breathe a little easier." June looked at Naomi's sleeping face and smiled. Her precious lips began to wiggle. "I'm going to go prep a bottle. She looks like she's going to wake up to eat pretty soon."

"Okay. I was thinking I'd go back to work tomorrow."

She stopped and turned around. "Already? It's only been two days."

"I know. But you don't really need me anymore, do you?"

Her heart began to race. Could she handle being alone all day with an infant? What if something went wrong? Her mouth was a desert. She'd have to do it eventually. Did it matter how soon? "I guess not."

He grinned. "That's what I figured. I got a couple of emails from work today and things aren't going as smoothly as they need to be right now. But I'll get up early and be home in the afternoon. You probably won't even notice I'm not here."

23

July dropped her car keys on the kitchen island and tugged open the fridge. She grabbed a cheese stick and an apple and bumped the door closed on her way into the den. Her lips curved as her gaze landed on Gareth asleep on the sofa, a book on his chest and the TV playing some sort of late night sci-fi movie. She clicked off the TV off and sat, biting into the crisp apple as quietly as she could. He didn't have to try and wait up for her. She told him that every year. But he insisted that he didn't mind. She wouldn't deny that it made her warm and gooey inside. How had she gotten so lucky?

What was he reading? She angled her head so she could see the spine. James Herriot. Again. What was it about that country vet that drew Gareth back to its pages time and again? He'd never seemed interested in veterinary medicine. It was always medical research with him. But the stories in *All Creatures Great and Small* seemed to call to him. He read the entire series at least once a year, sometimes more.

Hmm. She took another bite of apple and chewed. Maybe they should get a dog. She'd never had pets, nor felt any great need to have them. But Gareth could talk for hours about the goofy puppy he'd had growing up. They'd had a mutual agreement that pets would wait until their kids were old enough to help with the care. But now... maybe it was time. It would certainly help with loneliness during tax season. Of course, it made haring off on weekend adventures harder. You had to find hotels that were pet friendly, or a good pet sitter. Then there was the whole issue of housebreaking. But they certainly had a nice enough yard... she'd do some research.

She set the apple down on a paper on the coffee table. Was he drawing flowers? Odd. Gareth wasn't one to draw. She squinted at the lines and his cramped, messy writing. What on Earth was it? She shook her head and ripped open the string cheese.

"Hey." Gareth's eyes fluttered open and he ran a hand over his face. "What time is it?"

"Just after one. You could've gone to bed, you don't have to wait on the couch."

He sat up and picked up her apple, crunching into it. "Then I wouldn't hear you though. I like to see you when I can. Even if it's at one in the morning. How's it going?"

"Making progress. I got a handful of extension requests filed. But some of Geoff's clients are causing a ruckus. They're adamant that they shouldn't be penalized just because he was unethical. I don't really understand how an extension is a penalty, but I referred them on up. If they get reassigned to someone who can work them in, it'll be even better. But I suspect they'll just end up placated and I'll still be hustling through their taxes on the sixteenth. What about you? Anything exciting going on here?"

"Not really. I watched some building shows and some kind of shark-octopus-cow combination monster that was rampaging on sea and land. I don't know where they come up with these ideas, but they're so ridiculous they're kind of neat."

July laughed. "Only you."

"Can't be just me. They keep making them. There have to be a lot of people out there who enjoy a good B film. Maybe you're the odd one for thinking they're silly."

"It's possible. What's the picture?" She nodded toward the drawing on the table.

"Oh. That's... nothing." He leaned forward and flipped it over.

She frowned. Was he blushing? She yawned, her jaw popping. Whatever. She'd get him to tell her later. When she'd had more than eight hours of sleep in the last two days. "I should get to bed. I'm going to try and go in at six again. I've got half a dozen files that are complete that I should be able to get done before nine. Then I can call and have them come in for signatures and they'll be off my list. I did the math this afternoon..."

He chuckled. "Of course you did."

She narrowed her eyes. Smart aleck. "As I was saying...I did the math this afternoon and if I can clear six clients a day, I'll get everyone done and not have to shuffle any of my original clients into an extension. I really hate to do that to them if I can avoid it."

"If anyone can do it, you can." Gareth stood and held out his hand. After she took it, he pulled her against his chest and kissed her soundly. Tingles started in her toes and worked their way through her. Yeah, she was lucky to have him all right.

JULY RUBBED her eyes and pushed away from her desk. Coffee. She needed more coffee. She gathered the three files that were complete, save for client signatures, and headed toward the break room. She'd get a good jolt of caffeine and drop these at Lisa's desk out front. Then when her clients came in they could sign them and Lisa could put them straight into the mail.

"Morning." Lisa turned from the coffee machine with a bright smile.

"I was going to come see you after I got more coffee...is that fresh?" July nodded toward the carafe.

"Just finished brewing. Those files for me to mail?"

"The clients need to sign them first. But I told them to check in with you—I was hoping you'd be willing to handle that and then get them mailed. I don't need to see them unless there's a problem. I've gone over the papers on the phone with them, so there shouldn't be an issue. The one in the red folder should be bringing a check with him."

Lisa reached for the files. "I can handle that. And if they need you, I'll let you know. You doing okay?"

July shrugged. "You know how it is this time of year. I'm sleep-deprived and stressed, but I'll get through it."

"Let me know if I can help." Lisa saluted with the files as she left.

If only she *could* help beyond getting signatures and dropping things in the mail. But at least they had someone to handle that for them. Not all firms did. She refilled her mug and returned to her office.

Eight forty-five. She could take another five minutes for herself. She dialed June.

"Hey Jules."

"Hey. Thought I'd check in, see how you, Toby, and Naomi were doing." July turned in her chair and looked out her office window at the busy streets of Arlington.

"Hanging in. Toby went back to work today... so we'll see if I make it. So far so good. But it's only been a few hours." June chuckled, but July caught the edge of desperation in her sister's tone.

"You're going to do great."

"Thanks. How's tax season treating you?"

"Same as ever. But I had a thought last night—and maybe it was delusions of the sleep-deprived—but do you happen to remember what kind of dog Gareth had growing up?"

"Hmm. I remember him going on and on about the thing. What'd they call it? Mutt?"

July snickered. She'd forgotten that. "Yeah. But was that his name or the breed?"

"Maybe both? I honestly don't remember. Want me to ask Toby?"

"Would you? Then text me if he knows?"

"Sure thing. You getting a dog?"

Were they? It had seemed like a good idea last night, but now it was...less appealing. But it wouldn't be for her. "Maybe. I'm thinking it might be a good thing for Gar. But I want it to be a surprise, so make sure Toby doesn't spill the beans."

"Got it. Hey...any chance you're free for lunch?"

"Not today, sorry. Maybe tomorrow? I'll let you know."

"All right. Get back to work." June's voice was teasing.

"Yeah, yeah. Kiss my niece for me." July hung up and turned back to her computer. She could email her in-laws and ask about the dog, but Gareth's mom would probably end up spoiling the surprise. That woman couldn't keep her mouth shut about anything. July loved her, but she was an open book. No, she'd wait and see if June could find something out. It wasn't like they had to get the same kind of dog. But it was a place to start.

JULY STOOD and stretched her arms up over her head. Her shoulders cracked and her legs protested the movement after sitting for so long. She dropped her head back to stretch her neck. She needed to put in at least another hour—or whatever it took to finish up this client's file—before she could go home. She'd leave it in Lisa's inbox on her way out. But for now, she needed a break.

She took a quick lap around the offices, poking her head in to say hi to the others who were still there working away. Some of the accountants took their files home, but July got distracted too easily. It was better to put in the long hours and make sure she always had what she needed at her fingertips.

Back in her office, she spun the chair backwards and knelt in the seat, reaching around for her keyboard. Her back protested at first, then settled as the new position unkinked several knots. June had texted her that Toby thought the dog had been a sheltie. That sounded right. She opened a browser and typed in a search for breeders in the region. She scanned the results. How were you supposed to choose? July scrubbed a hand over her face. She obviously needed to do some research on how to buy a dog. Why couldn't it be easy? She didn't have time to do the research right now and she didn't want to wait on the dog.

With a sigh, she composed an email to her father-in-law. He was better at keeping secrets. Since they'd had dogs all the time that she'd known them, maybe he'd have some suggestions of what to do and where to start. She clicked send and returned to the tax paperwork.

Ninety minutes later, July flipped over the last page. She'd checked and double-checked it. Her client wasn't going to be pleased at the amount they owed, but maybe they'd take her advice on withholdings this year. She snorted. Unlikely. They balked every year when she made suggestions for changing anything. They were going to need to start doing estimated quarterlies though if they didn't change something. You couldn't continue to owe this much year after year without the government getting annoyed. The IRS liked to have their money as quickly as possible. Too bad they weren't as quick with their refunds.

She sent a quick email letting the client know the amount and instructions for the final steps they needed to take so it could get in the mail. She skimmed the unread messages in her inbox. Her father-in-law had already written back? Why was he up so late?

24

Gareth stared at the drawing of dandelions. Pastor Brown had been right, it wasn't as simple as he'd previously thought. Yes, July's change of heart had been the final blow that sent him over the edge, but as he'd prayed and thought about it... there were a lot of things to write on those roots. And even the process of writing them down had helped some. He grabbed the paper and got out of the car.

He rang the bell and looked out over the neighborhood. It was a quiet, unpretentious area that reflected Paul Brown's heart. Did the man even realize he was the pastor of a mega church? Obviously, at some level, he knew it. But it hadn't gone to his head. Amazing.

"Gareth. It's so good to see you." Mary Brown opened the door with a warm smile. "Come on in and have a seat in the office. Paul's finishing up a phone call in the den. Can I get you something? I made cookies this afternoon."

"A cookie would be great. Thanks."

"Coffee to go with it? I can put on a pot of decaf. Or tea?"

"Decaf, if you're sure it's not too much trouble."

"Of course not. You go on in. I'll be right back after I let Paul know you're here."

He watched her travel down the hallway before crossing into the office. He set his drawing face down on the couch next to him. No point in explaining it all to Mary when she came back with cookies. Though she probably wouldn't ask. His gaze swung over to the bookshelves. The titles were primarily theology and Christian living, but he spotted a few volumes of fiction in there as well. No James Herriot though. At least not immediately visible. Had Paul read those stories? Would he understand the pull of that simple life spent helping others to the best of your ability? Probably. That's what he did as a pastor, really. Or, at least, it wasn't much different.

"Sorry about that." Paul came in with a tray. He kicked the door closed behind him. "Let's put this on the sofa, if that's all right? I always think I should get a coffee table or something for in here but then it starts to feel crowded."

"This is good—we'll be closer to the cookies."

Paul frowned, a twinkle in his eye. "I hadn't thought of that. Maybe I should put it on my desk."

Gareth laughed and grabbed a warm snickerdoodle. The man knew how to put you at ease, that was for sure. "Have you read James Herriot?"

Paul's eyebrows lifted as he reached for a steaming mug. "That's an interesting start to a conversation. I never have, actually. Though I enjoyed the television series quite a lot. Why do you ask?"

Why had he asked? "I'm not sure. I've been re-reading it... it's my go-to comfort book. His life always seemed so meaningful and simple. Sometimes I wonder if I'm really doing what I'm supposed to be doing, you know?"

"I do." Paul studied Gareth over the top of his coffee. "It's natural to reexamine your life when you're facing a big mental shift like this, but don't do anything rash."

"I'm not planning to. I'm happy enough at my job—and I do know what I do matters, in the long run. We just don't always get to see the immediate results." Gareth shrugged. It wasn't as if he was having a mid-life crisis or anything. It had just been on his mind, so he brought it up. He picked up the flower drawing and offered it to Paul. "I did manage to do my homework. You were right... it's a worthwhile exercise."

Paul took the paper with a slight smile. "Hmm. More roots than you thought, I see."

"Yeah."

"You said it was worthwhile. Tell me about that." Paul extended the paper back to Gareth.

He folded the drawing in half and tucked it under his leg. "I've been blaming everything on July, and that's neither fair nor accurate. Honestly, the majority of the roots on there don't deserve for me to be irritated with them. It took me a while to come around to it, but I think who I'm really angry at is God."

Paul nodded and took a sip.

He wasn't going to say anything to that? No shocked exclamation or a protest that Gareth shouldn't be mad at God? Gareth let out a breath. "I'm not sure I've ever admitted that I'm mad at God before. I... it doesn't seem like something you should admit to... or even be. I mean, He's God. We're supposed to submit to His will, right?"

"Absolutely. But do you think it's His will that July miscarries and you don't have children? Is everything that happens in the world God's will?"

Gareth frowned. "Isn't it?"

"I don't believe so, no. Because if everything that happens is God's will, where's our choice? No—God created us with free will and ever since Adam and Eve exercised theirs and got kicked out of Eden, our choices, our sin, impacts all that we touch."

That made sense. Mostly. "Okay... then how do you tell? Do

you just assume bad things aren't God's will and good things are?"

Paul shook his head. "No. You have to look at the Scriptures and do a lot of praying. With infertility specifically, there are instances in the Bible where it's shown to be a direct result of God's intervention—just like there are instances of Jesus healing the sick by forgiving their sin. Disease can be a consequence of sin, but it isn't always. No one should ever leap to the conclusion that if you had a better relationship with God you wouldn't be going through whatever trial you're facing. At the end of the day, I believe this is something we won't know for sure on this side of heaven."

Great. Another part of life that didn't fall happily into a nice logical framework. "So what does that mean?"

"It means you live your life entrenched in the Bible and prayer, surrendering yourself to God and asking Him to reveal His will and direct your steps and, at the same time, you use the brain He gave you and the wisdom of Godly friends and mentors to help you." Paul leaned back and set his mug on the desk behind him. "As for being angry at God, go back and read the Psalms more carefully. David has quite a few angry rants in there. It's okay to be angry and cry out for respite—and answers—but then you need to listen and see what He says about it, too."

Gareth drummed his fingers on the side of his coffee cup. Why couldn't God just make it cut and dry? Or give you the option to get rid of your free will once you received salvation? Wouldn't that make it easier for everyone? Though that would probably kill the relationship aspect of things that Pastor Brown always brought into his sermons. You can't have a relationship with a robot. At least not any kind of relationship that's worth having. "All right. I'm going to have to talk to July about how I feel, aren't I?"

"You said it, not me." Paul reached across for another

cookie. "Maybe not immediately—it'd probably be good to get a handle on some of your anger first, make sure that you're in a place where you can *talk*, not accuse or yell."

Gareth took a deep breath. There was some time built in, at least. With July neck deep in taxes, he had another week to get his head straight. "Okay. I'll do what I can."

"You and July were both doing so well with communication when we stopped meeting in the fall. Remember those principles that we went over and pray—before, during, and after."

TOBY OPENED the door on the fourth knock. Naomi lay on his shoulder and he was bouncing up and down, patting her back while she wailed.

"Took a while... is this a bad time?" Gareth eased back a step. Visiting was one thing. Interrupting a tough night was another.

"Nah. Come on in. She's just got an air bubble and I can't get her to burp. June says I don't pat her hard enough, but I don't want to hurt her, you know?" Toby pushed the door open wider and nodded toward the living room.

Gareth didn't know, but it made sense. "Not hurting her is good."

"Hey, Gareth. Did you eat dinner?" June lay stretched out on the sofa, an arm over her face. She was the picture of exhaustion. "I can fix you something."

He hadn't eaten, banking on a meal here. But there was no way he was going to make her get up. He'd just drive through something on his way home. "I'm good. I had a snack at the Pastor's."

"Why were you at the Pastor's?" June shifted her arm so she could see him better. "Everything okay?"

"Oh. Um. I figured Toby would have filled you in." Gareth

shot a glance at his brother-in-law. Didn't normal couples tell each other everything? He hadn't said Toby couldn't.

"She knows most of it. I just hadn't gotten to the part about you seeing Paul. It's been a little hectic around here the past few days." Naomi let out an enormous burp, complete with what had to be a large portion of her stomach contents. Toby grimaced and pulled her away from his shoulder. "Here, June. I need to go change my shirt."

June snickered and scooted up a tiny bit. "Unless Uncle Gareth wants to hold her?"

"Is she safe now?" Gareth eyed the baby. She was quiet now. And seemed happy. He held out his arms. Clothes could be washed.

June tossed a larger-than-usual washcloth-like thing at him. "Here. Just 'cause her dad's too manly to use a burp cloth doesn't mean you have to be."

"I couldn't find it. I love burp cloths. I would dress completely in burp cloths if I could." Toby huffed out of the room.

Gareth kissed Naomi's forehead. "Good job, girlie. Get Daddy as often as you can."

"Careful. He finds out you're poisoning her against him, the gloves'll come off." June sat up and rolled her head around on her neck. "I'm glad you're talking to Pastor Brown though. Has it been helpful?"

"Yeah. Though I'm going to have to talk to July about things at some point. Probably sooner than later. At least now I'm starting to get a handle on my anger though. So maybe it'll help instead of causing a fight. I'm still not sure, but I'm warming up to the idea that it has to happen. Trying to bury it hasn't worked out all that well for me."

Toby padded back into the room wearing a clean shirt. "Spit up on Uncle Gareth. Show him how awesome that is."

Gareth chuckled. "You wouldn't do that to me, would you Naomi? No. No, of course you wouldn't."

Toby shook his head and plopped onto the couch next to June.

"How are you adjusting to parenthood? Getting the hang of things?" Gareth rubbed noses with Naomi.

"Getting there. I went back to work on Tuesday... it's harder than I thought it'd be to be gone all day." Toby frowned. "But they needed me—things are going crazy."

"It's not exactly a walk in the park to be here alone all day after dealing with her all night, too." June sighed. "It's harder than I realized it was going to be. She cries so much and I don't know if I'm doing something wrong or if that's just what she needs to do. But she only stops when I hold her. She really only sleeps when I hold her. And since I have to hold her to feed her... I pretty much hold her all the time until Toby gets home."

Gareth pursed his lips. That didn't sound bad to him, but it was clearly not how June was hoping things would be going. Did he want to ask? Not really. He had enough to deal with right now. "Uh... I'm sorry?"

"It's not your fault. It'll get better... it has to, right? It's just change." June shrugged. "You sure you don't need dinner?"

"Yeah, I'm sure. In fact, why don't I get out of your hair? Maybe Toby can hold her for a while and let you go take a nap or something? I don't know." Gareth handed Naomi to her dad and stood. "'Night. Hang in there."

25

June flopped back on the couch as Toby walked Gareth to the door. A nap would be heaven. But then she wouldn't sleep at night. Not that she was doing a ton of sleeping at night right now, just an hour here or there in between Naomi's feedings. It didn't seem to matter that she was exhausted; once she was up, her body took a long time to wind back down. By the time she was finally asleep again, Naomi was already starting to stir. Mom had been full of advice on the phone, but ignoring the noises before Naomi was truly awake and hungry wasn't as easy as it seemed when the baby in question was asleep on top of you. June had tried putting Naomi down in the crib but the baby simply wasn't having it. It didn't matter if Naomi was awake, drowsy, or completely asleep, the second June tried to walk away, her eyes flew open and she began howling. So, June had been sleeping—if you could call it that—holding Naomi in the rocking chair. It wasn't restful. What if she relaxed so much that she dropped the baby?

"Do you want to go upstairs and sleep for a bit?" Toby came back in and settled at the foot of the couch. "I can handle her for a while and let you have a break."

"I want to... but then I don't get to see you at all." Or have an adult conversation. That had also been in short supply since Toby went back to work.

He tipped his head to the side, his gaze meeting hers. "I'm not sure what the right thing to do here is, June. You've got to get more sleep than you're managing. I want to spend time with you, too, but not if it means you're going to be miserable and exhausted."

Wasn't that how you defined being a mom to a newborn? Miserable and exhausted? It sure seemed to fit her experience. June managed a weak smile. "All right, I'll go up for a bit. Thanks."

She pushed up off the couch and shuffled into the kitchen. She could at least prep all the bottles she'd need tonight. One less thing for Toby to have to manage on his own. Plus this way she wouldn't lay in bed worrying that he'd forget to do it. She filled four bottles with water and measured the formula powder into the handy container Toby'd found at the store. It had four segments that each held enough powder for one bottle and a lid that spun to let you dump one portion at a time into a bottle. It wasn't foolproof, but it was easier and faster than trying to scoop the powder in the middle of the night. Loading it all on the cookie sheet they used as a tray, she headed upstairs, pausing to kiss Toby and Naomi on her way through the living room.

HUNGRY CRIES WOKE HER. June reached to pat the baby and sat up, her heart pounding. Where was Naomi? The crying continued. June rubbed the sleep out of her eyes and looked around. Toby's gentle snores whuffled from the other side of the bed. She was in their room. How had Toby managed to get Naomi to sleep in her crib for even an hour?

Groggy and nauseated, June hauled herself out of bed and crept out of the bedroom, pulling the door closed.

"Shhh. Mommy's here, sweetie." June unscrewed the lid of the bottle and fumbled in the dark for the formula. After tapping the container to make sure the powder was all out, she screwed the nipple back on and double-checked that it wasn't crooked before beginning to shake it. She'd only had to shake a full bottle all over herself once before incorporating that double-checking step into her routine. There was nothing to compare to a tepid, smelly dousing in the middle of the night with a wailing baby who didn't understand what was taking so long.

She gathered Naomi out of the crib and kissed her forehead as she popped the bottle into her mouth. "There you go."

June smiled at the slurping sound. Her baby girl wasn't a delicate eater, that was certain. She settled into the rocking chair and hummed an old hymn, her own eyes drifting closed. She hovered in that half-asleep state, rocking back and forth, while the bottle grew lighter and the sucking quieter. She pried open an eye, pulled the bottle out of Naomi's mouth, and transferred her to her shoulder. Three pats and a solid rub later, the baby burped.

June chuckled. That was at least one thing she could do right. Why couldn't Toby manage it? He was a man—didn't that make him predisposed to more fully understand belching? She carried Naomi to the changing table and unsnapped her sleeper. She wasn't too wet, but a change now would wake her up enough to finish the bottle. Finishing the bottle would, in theory, lull her back to sleep.

Naomi whimpered.

"It's okay. Just a quick change and you'll be warm again, I promise." June wrapped up the diaper and dropped it in the pail. "All right, let's go finish that bottle and then maybe we can both get back to sleep. Did you like it in the crib when Daddy put you there? You going to go back to sleep there for Mommy? I'd really appreciate it."

Back in the rocker, Naomi's whimpers turned to wails. She flailed her tiny arms and legs and refused to close her mouth around the bottle. June jostled the nipple in Naomi's mouth.

"Shhh. Come on, sweetie, finish it up and you'll be happy again. And we'll sleep."

The wails escalated. How could something so small produce this much noise? June set the bottle aside and put Naomi on her shoulder, rocking and singing. Naomi heaved sobbing breaths. What was wrong?

June sang through as many hymns as she could remember. They were usually soothing, but tonight they didn't help either one of them. Her heart sank. Was it her? She should be able to calm a baby, shouldn't she? Anyone could do it. A real mother could. A tear slipped down her cheek, followed by another and another.

"Please stop, baby girl. I don't know what's wrong and I can't fix it. Shhh. You don't want to wake Daddy. He has to work."

Heat pumped off Naomi's body as she flailed and screamed. June tried walking around the room, a gentle bounce in her step. She sang, which seemed to only make the crying get louder, she rocked. Nothing helped. The clock on the dresser said it had been an hour.

"Why are you crying, baby? I don't know what to do." June sniffled back a sob. Maybe she wasn't cut out for this after all. "Stop. Please, stop."

She laid Naomi in her crib and stepped back. How did she manage to get even louder? June ran her hands through her hair. Now what? She couldn't just leave her here, screaming. But nothing she did made any difference. Toby. He was going to be annoyed. Didn't matter. She needed Toby.

June hurried to their room and shook Toby's shoulder.

"Hunh?" He sat up, rubbing his eyes. "Time's it?"

"Almost three-thirty."

He lay back down. "'K."

"No. Toby..." June shook him again. "I don't know what to do. She's just crying and crying and I..." Her voice broke into sobs and she buried her face in her hands. "I... can't... I... don't..."

Toby sat up, swung his feet to the floor, and pulled her closer. "I got it. You go to sleep."

"But you have to work and I should be able..."

"Shh. You're exhausted. Go to sleep, I'll get her."

Tears streaming down her face, June nodded and crawled under the covers. She buried her face in the pillow, sobs shaking her shoulders. She should be able to do this. Why was she so terrible at being a mother?

SUNLIGHT PEEKED around the edges of the bedroom blinds. June opened her eyes and stared at the ceiling. She should get up and check on Naomi. Heaviness settled over her limbs, pushing her further into the mattress. What if she couldn't soothe the baby again today, when Toby wasn't home to help? What was she supposed to do?

A light tap on the open door drew her attention. She turned her head. Toby smiled at her.

"I wondered if you were up yet. Feeling better?" He came in and sat on the edge of the bed.

No. She wasn't feeling better. How could she be? She was an absolute failure as a mother. It seemed there were reasons God hadn't let her conceive and now... now they had this precious baby and she was just going to mess it all up. She opened her mouth but the words lodged in her throat. She shrugged. "I guess. Less tired at least. How's Naomi?"

"She's fine. Taking a snooze after some very exciting tummy

time." He watched her for several heartbeats. "Need me to take today off?"

She did. She really did. But that would mean admitting her failure. And then what? Toby wasn't going to be the stay-at-home parent. Her job was good, but she didn't make as much as he did. Plus, she didn't love her job like he did. Maybe she was better at it than she was at being a mom but that wasn't saying a whole lot. "You don't have to do that. I'll be okay."

"You're sure?"

June sat up and stretched her arms over her head. "Sure. Can you let me get a shower first?"

"Of course. I'll go fix you some coffee."

She waited for him to leave before she hid her face in her pillow and sobbed.

26

"Hey. Got a minute?" June clamped the phone between her ear and shoulder and tiptoed out of the living room where Naomi napped fitfully in her bassinet.

"Only just. What's up?" July sounded distracted.

"Just checking in, really... seeing how you're doing. I know it's your busy time... going okay?" Should she not have called? "I won't keep you."

"No, it's okay. I can use a short break. Things are insane. I told you I got a whole bunch of clients dropped on me at the last minute and they're all up in arms that they may end up with extensions. Plus, the company's doing an internal audit on all of them to make sure we've weeded out all the people who were taking advantage of Geoff's willingness to do an end run around our ethics. So a couple of times when I thought I could squeeze one of his clients in, it turned out that instead I had to break the news to them that we'd be reporting fraud on their account."

June winced. "That sounds... horrible."

"Yeah, basically. I'll get through it, but I'm looking forward to the sixteenth. Not that the way things are going that's going to make as much a difference as most years, but at least I'll have some breathing room. So how are you?"

"Exhausted. Naomi cries so much. She only sleeps when she's being held and I'm so worried about squishing her if I bring her into bed with us that I've been sleeping in the rocking chair. Which isn't that conducive to sleeping, truth be told. And it's just... hard. By the time Toby gets home I'm clinging to sanity by the ragged edges of my fingernails."

"Colic?"

Was that what it was? "I guess. Honestly, I've been so frazzled I haven't really put any thought into what it could be."

"Google colic and see what turns up. How's Toby doing back at work?"

Really? That was it? June leaned against the kitchen counter and blinked back the tears that burned her eyes. "Okay, I guess. I... Jules..."

"What?"

Her shoulders slumped. "Never mind. I'll let you go."

"Don't be silly. What?"

"I guess I hoped you'd be a little sympathetic... or understanding... or something." Her voice broke.

Silence stretched over the line for several heartbeats. July cleared her throat. "I'm sorry you're having trouble, but you wanted this—paid a lot of money for it, even."

Hot tears dripped down June's cheeks. July wasn't wrong... but was it too much to ask for her sister to offer some support? Apparently it was. She swallowed. "You're right. I'll let you get back to work."

June put the phone down on the kitchen island and scrubbed at the tears that continued to fall. Nobody understood. Toby just hurried off to work in the morning and told her to take a nap when he got home. July acted like it wasn't okay to struggle with adjusting to the whole thing. She wiped her nose across her shoulder. Maybe she was just a big baby... but was it really supposed to be this hard? Everyone painted motherhood as this blissful union of souls—love that consumed you from the inside out the minute your eyes met your child's. Instead of that, June had a screaming, flailing baby that had to be constantly held. And that didn't even soothe her. If she was supposed to be a mom, shouldn't this be easier?

~

"You look terrible." Lydia shouldered past June and tromped down the hall.

"Gee, thanks. It's great to see you, too." June frowned and closed the door, following her friend into the kitchen. "I was hoping for a pick-me-up when I invited you to lunch. Not another kick in the teeth."

Lydia set the plastic take-out bags on the island and held open her arms. "I'm sorry. It's been rough?"

June nodded and let Lydia hug her. Tears pricked her eyes and she hauled in a deep breath. She'd sobbed entirely too much already today, she wasn't going to start again. "Thanks for bringing lunch."

"Happy to. Especially since it means I get to snuggle your baby girl before Sunday. I'd been trying to decide if I should force myself on you this week. Kevin convinced me that maybe some adjusting time would be a good thing." Lydia cocked her head to the side. "Maybe that was the wrong decision."

"I didn't expect..." A wail split the air. "That. That's practically all she does unless you're holding her. I put her down ten minutes ago so I could go to the bathroom... but that's six minutes longer than my last record. So things are improving?"

"Go get her. I'll bring lunch that way." Lydia started opening cabinets. "Shoo. I'll find what I need."

Shoulders drooping, June went into the den and took Naomi out of the bassinet. "Shh. There's my girl."

Naomi stopped crying mid-wail when June settled her into her arms and wiped the fat tears off her cheeks. Naomi's crystal blue eyes locked on June's face. Something stirred in June's chest and she kissed the baby's head. "I love you, Naomi. It's not what I thought it was going to be... but we'll get there... right?"

"Of course you will." Lydia slid two plates onto the coffee table. "Can you sit, or does she make you stand, too?"

June lowered to the couch. "She doesn't care, provided she's being held."

Lydia held out her arms. "Then hand her here and you go ahead and eat. I'll eat when you're finished."

June eyed the plate of pasta salad. Her mouth watered. She transferred Naomi to Lydia and pulled the plate into her lap. A smile tugged at the corner of her mouth as Lydia began to coo at Naomi. What was it about babies that brought out the silly in adults? Or at least most of them—her sister was a bizarre exception. "So how have you been? Everything still progressing like it should be?"

"I had a sonogram the other day. I'm not far enough along to tell gender or anything, but you can see the unmistakable shape of a baby." Lydia grinned. "Everything's right where it's supposed to be. I'll be twelve weeks soon... I'm almost at the point where I can exhale."

"Kevin?"

"He's having a hard time not shouting it from the mountaintops. I think we're both past the point of cautiously optimistic now, but neither wants to be the first to say something. It's pathetic, really. We don't believe in luck, but..." Lydia shrugged and rubbed her nose to Naomi's.

June took a bite of pasta and nodded. "I understand that.

Toby and I are kind of in the same situation. She's not ours, not officially, until Monday at the earliest. We've already had one scare and we're both holding our breath until the papers are signed."

"What happened?"

June filled Lydia in on the trip to the adoption agency to meet Betty. "In the end, it was a good thing and I'm glad we got a chance to know a bit about her and give her the reassurance she was looking for, but at the time I was ready to curl up in a ball and die. The whole drive there I was convinced we wouldn't be leaving with Naomi."

"Wow."

June set her empty plate aside and reached for the baby. "Here, let me have her so you can eat."

"How's July doing with everything?" Lydia stabbed a forkful of pasta salad.

"I don't know. She was here on Sunday for Easter and she took care of Mom and Dad while we ran off to the hospital but when we got back, she wouldn't hold Naomi and she hasn't even called to check in all week. I know she's crazily busy at work—tax season—but I just... I guess I thought she'd be more interested in her niece than this. I called her this morning and was trying to explain how hard it's been and she pretty much said that this is what I volunteered for so I'm not allowed to complain." June scooted Naomi over to lie on her shoulder. "Maybe she's right. I mean it's not like this was a big accident."

"She's not right." Lydia set down her fork and frowned. "But I think she's reacting from a place of hurt. She and Gareth aren't adopting, right?"

June shook her head. "No. But that's July choice. I'm not sure Gareth's thrilled about it."

"Doesn't matter whose choice it was. The fact is that she's officially never going to be a mother and she's going to have to deal with that. Even if she says she's happy about it, I'm guessing she's still hurting. And if Gareth isn't totally reconciled to not adopting, that's just going to make it worse because she likely can't explain any of her feelings to him because she isn't sure how he'll respond. Which isn't to say she should've said that to you—she was out of line. But you should try and understand where she's coming from, too."

June sighed. That made sense. Mostly. But why was she always the one who had to end up putting herself in someone else's shoes? "Yeah, I guess."

Lydia pointed her fork at June. "It's not fun being the grown up, but we all have to do it."

"Fine." June shook her head and fought a smile. "I'm so glad you came over."

"Let's hope you still feel that way after I give you this." Lydia pulled a folded piece of paper out of her back pocket. "From what you said on the phone when you called... I thought this might help. We use it at the Pregnancy Center."

June took the paper and smoothed it out. The baby blues? "I didn't give birth, I can't have post-partum depression."

"Here's the thing... I talked with Maureen, the director at the Center, and she said it's actually not uncommon for adoptive parents—moms in particular—to have post-partum. Particularly if the baby is colicky. You're going through a lot of changes, coupled with sleep deprivation and stress. Depression is a natural response to that."

June pursed her lips and looked down at the brochure.

"Maureen also mentioned, though I'm sure you already know it, that bonding takes awhile, even for biological parents. So you shouldn't be down on yourself if you're not feeling the throes of ecstasy every time you look into Naomi's eyes. It'll come."

June's eyes filled with tears as the invisible weight that had been pressing down on her lifted. "Really?"

"Really. I can't speak from personal experience yet, but I trust Maureen."

"Okay." She set the brochure aside. "I'll look at that later. Thanks."

"Still glad I came?"

"Absolutely."

27

"Knock, knock."

July looked up from her computer screen. "Hey, honey. What brings you here?"

"It's Friday night. Figured I could at least have dinner with my wife, even if she has to work late. You've gotta eat, right?"

She smiled and stretched her arms over her head, causing several joints to pop. "I do. You just made my day."

"Where can I set this?" Gareth held up a bag.

July looked at her desk. The piles were jumbled, but she knew where everything was. It would take too long to reorganize in a reasonable way that left enough room for two people to eat. "Um."

"Carpet picnic?" Gareth reached into the bag and pulled out a tablecloth. "I planned ahead, just in case."

"Perfect. Just move those chairs out of the way. Let me finish this thought while you set up."

Gareth nodded.

She turned back to her computer and rapidly entered numbers into the form, double-checking the totals as they accumulated. Too bad there wasn't a 'Husband of the Year' award. Gareth definitely deserved a nomination. She clicked save and pushed away from the desk. "What can I do?"

"Just have a seat." Gareth patted the floor.

Chuckling, July slipped off her shoes and sat, folding her legs under her. "This was a great idea. You're the best."

Gareth grinned and handed her a takeout container. "I didn't bother with plates and such—do I lose points for that?"

July popped open the container and breathed in the heady aroma of spices wafting up from the gyro that sat nestled on an enormous Greek salad. "Nope. You drove across town to get this, which makes up for eating out of Styrofoam any day."

"I thought you might be tired of all the places within walking or delivering distance."

She nodded and took a bite, the savory lamb exploding across her taste buds. She licked a drip of tzatziki sauce before it could ooze out of the corner of her mouth. "Mmm. Heaven."

Gareth took a bite of his own. "So how's it going? You gonna make it?"

"It's getting there. It'll be tight, but yeah, I think I'm in a good place. I might even be able to swing church on Sunday before coming in. I'd like to." It'd be nice to have a chance to do something normal and forget, if only for a few hours, that it was the middle of tax season.

"Cool." He paused but didn't meet her gaze. "I was going to try and wait until you were done with this craziness before bringing this up but maybe now is better."

July's mouth went dry. She swallowed, the food sticking in her throat. Her stomach dropped to her toes. "Okay?"

"You know how I said I understood about you not wanting to adopt?"

She nodded.

He looked down at his food and cleared his throat. "I don't. Not really. I've been trying to, but I can't wrap my head around it. You were so determined to conceive. I thought that was because you were determined to have a family. That's why I went along with it, because I thought our dreams were the same and we were just working on two different ways to get there. But then, *boom*, you're just done? I don't—I can't—how did you do such a fast about-face?"

July licked her lips. Why had he said he understood if he didn't? She crushed her teeth together and jerked her chin up. "Why'd it take so long for you to say something? It's been over a month."

"Because I knew you'd be angry. Like you are." Gareth sighed. "I don't like fighting with you... especially after last fall. I was hoping I could figure out a way to get over it. Move on. Be okay. But..."

She pressed her lips together. She had to try and see his side of things. Wasn't that what the Browns had said? But if he didn't want something, wouldn't she lay her own preferences aside and go along with it? Her cheeks heated. Apparently not. Because he did want something and she'd grabbed on to her own wants and pushed his out of the way. She blew out a breath. "I hear what you're saying... and I probably haven't handled this right... but Gar, none of that changes how I feel. Every time we talk about adopting, I start to feel ill. I just—I can't."

He stared at her before giving a slow nod. "All right. Will you come talk to the Pastor with me? Or go see him on your own?"

Really? He had to drag the Browns back into this? "Are you going to run to them every time we have a disagreement from now on? That's ridiculous. Why would we need to talk to the Browns?"

"You have a better solution? I'm trying so hard to keep this from turning into another crazy fight, Jules. But I don't understand where you're coming from—I hear what you're saying, but I don't get the *why* of it. And you're in the same boat, right?

I thought I could just give in, let you have your way, but it's eating me up inside."

"So *you* go talk to the Pastor. Have him help you figure out how to get over it." July crossed her arms. She wasn't going to bring the Pastor back into their marriage just because Gareth was too stubborn to back down and accept that things changed. It didn't matter if she was just as stubborn, she was *right*.

"I already have. He said I needed to talk to you about how I was feeling. I told him this would happen." Gareth shook his head and flipped the lid of his container closed. "I'll get out of your hair. I know you're busy and this probably wasn't the best time to try to talk to you."

Timing wouldn't have changed anything. Why couldn't he understand that? "Gareth..."

"Don't, okay?" He stood and collected his side of the picnic area. "I don't want to argue when there's no chance of either of us getting through to the other. I'm tired of that. I'll see you when you get home tonight."

July watched him leave. Should she ask him to stay? Force a conversation? To what end? He was right—neither one of them was likely to change their minds simply because they kept hammering at the subject. She closed her takeout box and swallowed back her rising nausea. Maybe she'd be able to eat later, after her stomach untwisted itself.

JULY SAGGED against the garage door. The light over the kitchen sink was on, but the rest of the main floor looked dark. Had Gareth gone to bed? She checked the time on the oven—it was almost two in the morning. Maybe it wasn't unreasonable for him to be sleeping. She usually made it home before one, but after the dinner fiasco... she hadn't been able to make herself hurry. Gareth wasn't the only one tired of arguing.

Dropping her purse on the floor, she slipped out of her shoes and padded through the living room on her way upstairs. Gareth lay on the couch, a blanket tucked under his chin, leaving his toes poking out. Soft snores filled the room. July smiled. Even when he was driving her crazy, she couldn't escape the fact that he was everything she'd prayed for in a husband and then some. They'd find their way through this. They had to.

She inched closer. *Crinkle.* What was that? She looked down. Several balled up pieces of paper littered the floor. She knelt and collected them. He was probably sketching chemical compositions or something for work. She was always finding doodles of various elements and compounds in the margins of notes he left her. A hazard of being married to a researcher, most likely. July brushed her lips across the top of his head, careful not to wake him. Carrying the paper balls and her shoes, she went upstairs.

She tossed the paper into the trashcan in their room and disappeared into the closet. At least tomorrow she could sleep in and wear comfortable clothes to the office. Why they didn't lift the dress code in the office during tax season was one of the mysteries she and her coworkers discussed during hurried lunches in April. The taxes would get filed regardless of what she wore, and jeans would make the long hours more bearable. She hung up her slacks and blazer. At least pantsuits were an option these days. Wearing stockings for eighteen hours wasn't something she ever wanted to experience.

Clad in her pajamas, she flipped off the bathroom light and jumped. "You startled me."

Gareth offered a tired smile. "Sorry. I didn't hear you come in. I tried to wait up."

"I'm later than usual... I should have called." She winced.

"S'okay."

She studied him. Was there more he wasn't saying? "I love you."

He kissed her forehead. "Love you, too."

With a slight frown, she followed him back into the bedroom and flipped down her covers. Tension melted away as she lay down. Should she bring up dinner and try to have a conversation about it now? Rolling to her side, she yawned. Gareth snuggled up behind her, his arm curving around her waist, pulling her close. Warmth flooded her. Any conversation they needed to have would keep until tomorrow. And maybe a few hours of rest would help her know what to say.

28

"I was thinking maybe we should get a dog." July looked across the kitchen table at Gareth.

"You hate dogs."

"Hate's a strong word... I just never had one before."

What was this about? A dog wasn't a baby. Was it some sort of consolation prize? "What brought this on?"

She sighed across the top of her coffee. "I started thinking about it a while ago. I knew something was up with you—it wasn't until last night that I understood what the problem was though. And I know it's not the same thing as agreeing to rush out and adopt but maybe... I don't know, maybe it would help me somehow."

That made no sense. How was getting a dog going to help her want to adopt? Or was she saying it'd help her by convincing him that he didn't want kids because they had a dog? That didn't seem likely either. Gareth frowned. "I'm not following."

"Never mind. Maybe it's a stupid idea." July shoved back her chair. "I should get going. I'll try to be home earlier tonight."

July fled. That was really the only word for how quickly she left. He should've said something. But what? A dog would be great... but only if she was on board, really on board. Dogs were a lot of work. And in that way they were a lot like kids... so if she wasn't interested in anything but biological kids why was he still pushing for them?

He grabbed the phone when it started to ring.

"Hello?"

"Hi Gareth, honey. It's Mom."

He grinned. It didn't matter how many times he explained that he'd know her voice anywhere, Mom still made a point of saying who it was. "Hey, Ma. How are you?"

"Oh you know how it is. Your father is out messing around in the garden. He has some grand plan to grow enough zucchini to feed a small foreign country or something. I don't know why the man insists on planting more than one of those things. Neither of us actually like it. Well, unless it's in bread. But really, how much zucchini bread can a body eat? Still, he says gardening relaxes him. So I'll just keep baking bread and leaving packages on neighbor's stoops in the middle of the night."

Gareth chuckled. Did she dress up like a Ninja to deliver those baked goods to all the neighbors in the dark? Or did she sneak past their motion sensor lights with her hair in curlers? "Can't you get him to grow tomatoes or something?"

"Oh, don't mention the tomatoes. We'll be up to our ears in marinara sauce by the end of the summer, too. Anyway. I didn't actually call to talk about your father's garden. I've been emailing with July a bit over the last few weeks about dogs and she just replied to my last suggestion and I got the feeling that everything might not be all right with you two."

Gareth grabbed his empty mug and headed to the counter for a refill. "It's a long story, Ma."

"Did I not mention your father's in the garden? I've got nothing but time."

He carried his coffee into the living room and sank into the recliner, summarizing the bare bones for his mother. He left out all the online bits, no sense in rehashing that. Not to mention he could only imagine what she'd have to say about it. He finished with their conversation about the dog this morning.

"Oh, honey. I was worried it was something like that. You've got to understand her side of things."

Had July been talking to his mom? "I'd love to, but she doesn't explain it. All she says is that she can't face adopting. But why not? What's the hang up?"

"I don't know for certain, but adoption isn't for everyone. You have to realize that. Maybe she's worried about the cost? Or the uncertainty of waiting? Or just having other people perceive her as less of a parent than a biological parent? Or something completely different. But if she's not comfortable, you know you need to stop pushing."

"I haven't pushed, Ma. Until last night, I don't think she even knew I was upset. Or why I was upset. Apparently she noticed something was bothering me, though, and thought a dog would fix it." Gareth sipped his coffee. Why was he always the one who had to be wrong?

"I don't think it was quite like that. You hurt her feelings this morning when you rejected even the idea of getting a dog. She's trying to reach out. I know it's not exactly what you want, but maybe, if you stop and think about it, you'll see that a dog might be a good first step anyway. It's no guarantee that she'll want to adopt down the line, but it's not going to make it less likely. And in the meantime, you'd have a dog to cuddle. Just think about it, okay?"

"Yeah. Okay." He frowned. Maybe he'd overreacted, but the dog thing had come out of left field. "Out of curiosity, what did you suggest to her?"

"I'll forward you the email."

GARETH SQUATTED by the cage at the end of a row. The bare fluorescent bulbs overhead flickered. He looked in and smiled. A black and brown puppy was curled in a ball at the back of the cage, one paw over its nose as it slept.

"Any idea on the mix?"

The shelter worker shook her head. "Not really. We can run DNA if you decide to adopt her. Given her coat and markings though, I'd say there's some Lab in there. Maybe a little Australian Shepherd?"

Gareth pursed his lips. Lab and Aussie would make a pretty big dog. Not enormous, but a good size. Of course, being female, she'd be on the smaller end of big, but still. Would July be okay with that? Most of the rescues and shelters his mom had suggested were Sheltie-heavy. As much as he'd enjoyed their dog growing up, he wanted something bigger. A man dog.

The dog stirred, her mouth opening in a tongue-lolling yawn. Brown eyes popped open and met his. She jumped to her feet, her entire back half wagging as she raced to the front of the cage and thrust her nose through the openings.

"As you can see, she's very friendly. We figure she's probably six months old. Someone found her wandering around in bad shape, no collar or evidence that she'd ever had medical care. They brought her here. We've done all her basic shots and so forth. She's too young yet to spay, but your agreement to do that would be required as part of her adoption."

"She's perfect." Gareth scratched the puppy's nose. He was sunk the minute those eyes had latched on to his own. "Can I take her out and hold her?"

"Sure." The woman looked down the row of mostly empty cages as a phone rang in the distance. "I'll be right back. Go ahead and play with her a bit, get to know her."

Gareth unhooked the latch. The puppy tumbled into his lap

and stood on her hind legs, her white-striped nose bumping his before she began to bathe his face with sloppy kisses. He laughed and ran his hands down her sides, pausing to scratch behind her ears and on her rump. She wiggled and yipped. "Hey girl. You're a beauty, aren't you? Can you pose for me?"

He slid his cell phone out of his pocket and snapped a picture. Grinning, he texted it to July. "That's a girl. You're happy, too, aren't you?"

His phone rang.

"That was fast."

July cleared her throat. "Yeah, well... I'm surprised, I guess. It doesn't look like the pictures of shelties I looked up online though."

Gareth chuckled. "It's not. They're thinking aussie/lab mix, but they don't know. So she'd be bigger than a sheltie. Maybe fifty pounds? I'll ask, but it'd only be a guess on their part anyway."

"Who's they?"

"Oh. The shelter. Mom called and after she read me the riot act about my reaction to the dog thing this morning—I'm sorry, by the way—she forwarded me the email she'd sent you with some suggestions from her rescue friends. I visited a few, but as much as I loved our dog Prince growing up..."

"You want something different. I can understand that. I'll admit I like the look of this one's coat better than the shelties I saw. All that hair."

He nodded. Grooming a sheltie could be a full-time job. This girl had a coat much more like a Lab—lots easier to maintain. "Do you want to meet her? Or..."

"Or what?"

"Well, if you were serious about getting a dog and you like her picture and are willing to trust me... I'll just take her home."

"You're serious."

He winced. "We can wait. I just worry someone else'll come and grab her. She's so sweet. But there are other dogs that I'm sure are just as great, and if you need me to wait until after you get all the taxes done, I understand."

There was a pause while keyboard tapping filled the line. "Can you give me thirty minutes? I need a break anyway. Why don't I load up a bag with files, grab my laptop, and meet you there? Then if we end up taking her home, I can hang out and work there for the rest of the day while we get her settled."

"Really? Sounds great. See you soon." He tucked the phone back in his pocket as the puppy licked his chin. "Hear that, girl? Mommy's on her way here. She doesn't know it yet, but you're ours. Yes, you are."

"I take it that means I should go start the paperwork?"

Gareth shook his head at the woman's amused smile. "Maybe not quite yet. My wife's on her way here. I should probably let her think she has a choice."

"Fair enough. If you want to bring her up front, you can wait for your wife in the lobby. It's more comfortable than the concrete."

MILLIE HOPPED onto the couch and curled into a ball on his legs, her chin resting on his knee. Her eyes drifted shut but her ears remained perked, their flopped tips twitching. Gareth smiled. July had fallen in love as quickly as he had and Millie had spent the afternoon exploring the house, always running back for a scratch between the ears before much time had passed. She'd even managed to make it outside to do her business. Well, except for the first time. But really, a new home was exciting enough to warrant a one-time pass, wasn't it?

Now, as July continued hammering away at her laptop in the dining room, Gareth studied their new addition. Something in his heart had eased with each puppy lick. He wouldn't go so far as to say he was okay with the possibility of never having kids but it didn't seem like his heart had been sawn in half anymore either.

"She looks happy." July padded into the living room and sat on the edge of the coffee table.

"Yeah. And worn out. I guess exploring your new digs will do that." He met July's gaze. "This was a good idea. Thank you."

July's lips curved faintly. "I know it doesn't solve things..."

"No. But it helps. And I can shelve it for a while. For as long as you—we—need."

She slanted her head to the side. "What if I never change my mind?"

He closed his eyes. It wasn't a possibility he wanted to entertain, regardless of how realistic it might be. "Then we'll just have to pray that God will change mine. Even if we're not on the same page with this right now, Jules, we're okay. I—can we both agree to give it some time before we make our decision permanent?"

"All right." She leaned forward and kissed him. "You don't have to stay up. I'm going to work another hour, two tops. I want to get up and go to church tomorrow. I think I have enough with me to work from home afterward again."

"I'll wait a bit. If nothing else, I want to take Millie out one more time before bed. Try to reduce the necessity of taking her out in the middle of the night."

July chuckled. "Good luck with that."

29

June hovered outside the door to the classroom where their small group met. Her fingers clenched on the handle of the baby carrier. She looked at Toby and bit her lip. "Can we really take her in there?"

"Why couldn't we? Last year everyone had babies in here— some of them until they were practically six months old. Why would anyone mind?"

"I minded." June looked down at Naomi, her face peaceful in sleep, having just finished a bottle in the car. "It hurt. A lot. July minded too. Didn't you mind, even a little?"

Toby sighed and ran a hand through his hair. "All right, yeah. But... we were struggling. No one else has mentioned anything like that."

June arched a brow. They'd never mentioned their struggles either. Not really. Hanging out, sharing their pain with Lydia and Kevin was one thing, but they hadn't said anything to the class. Lydia must have mentioned it though, because the babies had trickled out of the room pretty quickly.

"What do you want to do? Go home? I thought you wanted to come to class."

"I do. I'm just... conflicted. July's already having a hard time with this. Is bringing Naomi to class going to make it harder? And I sure don't want to put anyone else in the same situation we were in."

Toby jammed his hands in his pockets. "So... what are we doing?"

"Going in. We're going in." June huffed out a breath and stepped through the doorway.

Lydia grinned from across the room and made a beeline for them. "You came! I wasn't sure you would. I know it's tricky taking the little ones out when they're so new. Kevin's been annoyed that he hasn't gotten a chance to hold her yet though."

Toby chuckled. "Then we'll have to give him a chance. She's snoozing right now, but I'm sure she'll wake up before long."

"Are you sure it's okay that we're here? I don't want..."

Lydia shook her head. "You're not going to. Come in and sit down."

Toby kissed June's cheek and veered toward a clump of men on the far side of the room.

"Are you feeling any better?" Lydia's voice was nearly a whisper.

June shrugged. "I guess. It helps, some, to know that it's normal. But I can't help feeling like I should just get over it. You know?"

Lydia pursed her lips. "Don't be too hard on yourself. Big changes, remember. These are big changes. Throw in sleep deprivation and the uncertainty of the placement until all the papers are signed and you're one hundred percent allowed to be struggling. But also keep in mind that your family and friends are here for you. You don't have to do this on your own."

"Thanks. I just wish..." June trailed off. There was no point in even finishing the sentence. Wishes weren't going to make July okay with things. They weren't going to make it not July's busiest time of year when they might actually have a chance to work things out more quickly. Nor were wishes going to help Toby understand that she really needed him at home still, regardless of the fact that she was going to have to manage on her own eventually.

"You wish?"

"Never mind. It'll be okay. I just keep telling myself that. Maybe, hopefully, sometime soon I'll believe it."

Lydia slung an arm around June's shoulder and squeezed.

The room filled with couples. June waved to them as they all took seats. Most came over to peek into the carrier and exclaim over Naomi before hurrying back to sit as Kevin called the class to order. July and Gareth slipped in at the end of his opening prayer and pushed chairs into the circle next to June and Toby with whispered greetings.

When class ended, several of the women from the class surrounded June.

"Congratulations. She's precious." Ginger perched on the chair next to June. "And now that you've adopted, you know you'll get pregnant."

Several heads bobbed in agreement.

"I have two friends who had that happen. It's all about getting rid of the stress. Hope you're ready for her to have an Irish twin."

June looked at the woman and tried to pull up her name. Didn't matter. Not really. She was clearly an idiot. Even if it had happened to two of her friends, how was that possibly encouraging? What would make her say that to someone? June offered a stiff smile. "If that's what God chooses to do, we'll roll with it."

July laid her hand on June's leg and gave a squeeze.

June's gaze darted to her sister. She saw the understanding gleam in July's eye. *Better part of valor. Focus on the better part of valor.* She let the chattering wash over her, giving only small nods when pauses seemed to require them. Were people really this clueless? Yes, having a baby now was wonderful—an amazing blessing. But it didn't magically erase the pain of the last year. Nor did it suddenly answer all the questions. She was still broken. Her body was still liable to pack on the pounds if she even thought about food. The only difference was now she'd have a child while it was going on.

"Will you tell her?"

The same woman—what *was* her name—spoke. June blinked. "Tell her?"

"That she's adopted? She looks enough like you, you probably don't have to. It's not like she's a different nationality."

Her jaw dropped. Coherent thought flew out the window for several heartbeats. She took a deep breath and cleared her throat. "Uh, no, we'll tell her. We don't want her to ever not know she was adopted. It's part of her history. I... I don't think people try to hide that anymore."

The woman shrugged. "Just wondering."

"Are you headed to the service now, or did you go already?" July leaned down and tucked the blanket more snugly under Naomi's chin.

"We're going to head home. She's probably going to want to eat again soon and I don't want to be the person with the screaming kid in the middle of the sermon. At least not yet."

"It'll happen eventually, I imagine." July grinned.

"More than likely. Remember when Dad had you on one side and me on the other marching down the center aisle in the middle of the service? You were saying hi to everyone we passed and I was already crying 'cause I knew we were getting spanked."

"Yeah. But he was such a soft-touch, he never really meant it. Mom...you didn't want to get her mad enough to haul you out though." July chuckled. "I guess Gareth and I will head out too. I should get back to work, though I'm making progress. I might even be able to squeeze in a few more completed returns if this keeps up. Do you have time for lunch?"

JUNE STRETCHED out on the couch and rocked the baby carrier with one hand. "Did you get an ear full of asinine comments at church like I did?"

"Probably not. I don't think guys do that. Mostly they just said congratulations and asked if I was going to start stockpiling shotguns for when she wants to date later."

She snickered. "Lucky. Apparently adopting a child will make my body function now. So never mind that a nationally known reproductive endocrinologist has decreed I'm never going to conceive, I'm now going to get pregnant. With twins."

Toby arched a brow. "Someone said that?"

"Essentially. Whatever. I mean, if God decides to work that way, then hey, great. But I probably won't run around shouting that that's what happened. It's like they don't have a clue how hurtful that is."

"They don't." Toby picked up her feet and sat. He began rubbing tiny circles in her arches. "I have to believe they think they're being encouraging. I'm beginning to suspect that people have either been through it—or something close enough—or they're clueless."

"Someone should write a book."

"You think anyone would read it? At least if they haven't been through it themselves?"

"Oh, who knows? But at least the people whose hearts are aching could throw a copy at the well-meaning people in their lives. Maybe that'd help."

He shook his head. "Unlikely. People like to live in their bubbles. They only leave when their own pain pops them. Someone else's pain isn't their problem."

"I guess." She frowned, her hand stilling. "Did you see the photo of Millie?"

"I did. She's adorable. You think July has any idea how big that dog's going to be though?"

"Not one." June smiled. "But since she's already pretty much in love with the pup, it's not going to matter... do you think it's going to help?"

Toby was quiet. After a moment, he lifted a shoulder. "I don't know. I hope so... but there's still so much they need to work through... it's hard to imagine this fixing things, but maybe it'll get them on the right path."

"July actually touched Naomi today. She didn't hold her, but she let Naomi grab her finger."

"It's a start. She'll come around. She's hurting too, whether or not she realizes it."

"I know." It didn't make it easier. Not really. But she was getting better at putting herself in her sister's shoes.

30

Gareth knocked on Pastor Brown's front door and tucked his hands in his pockets.

Paul answered with a smile and stepped back. "Come on in, Gareth. How are things going?"

"Pretty well, actually."

"Wonderful, wonderful. Have a seat and tell me about it." Paul gestured to the office.

"I talked to July on Friday and laid everything out for her."

"And it went well?"

Gareth shook his head. "Not really, no. It went about as badly as I'd imagined it would. Maybe slightly better, but not much."

Paul lifted his brows. "Okay?"

"Clearing the air was a good thing, turns out. Do you ever get tired of being right?" He waved away the question. "Don't answer that. Anyway, Saturday morning July says how she thinks we should get a dog."

"A dog."

"Right. Um, I guess I need to explain that July really doesn't care for dogs. They didn't have pets growing up and she had a bad experience being chased by a Doberman when she was eight or nine. So getting a dog is a big stretch for her. I guess she was talking to my mom about it for a while—maybe since she decided, we decided, that we weren't going to pursue adoption."

"So you got a dog?" Paul propped an ankle on his knee.

Gareth frowned. "Not immediately. I was...annoyed, I guess, with the suggestion. But then I talked to my mom—well, Mom called because I guess July texted her after our conversation about dogs—and Mom helped me realize that I hadn't been entirely fair about this whole thing."

Paul nodded.

"So I went and looked at some of the rescues Mom had suggested to July... and I found Millie."

The pastor grinned. "You sound like a man in love."

Gareth nodded and pulled out his phone. He flipped to the photos of the brown and black puppy and offered them to Paul. "She's the sweetest thing. I called July. I figured she'd say to do whatever I wanted, but she came to the shelter and really involved herself in the decision. Millie's good for both of us, I think. I—it doesn't ache quite so much. I'm not sure it'll ever go completely away, but Millie helps."

"And July? Has she said anything about it?"

"Actually... she agreed that we could just go back to saying adoption's on hold, rather than off the table. I, in here," Gareth tapped his chest, "I know she's not going to change her mind. But the fact that she's willing to pray about it more with me, that means something. So I've been praying that God would fill the hole. And maybe it's not exactly getting filled, but it feels less like a cavern these days. So that's something."

"That's a big something." Paul scratched his chin. "It's not exactly what I imagined, but it sounds like the way God works. And as a side benefit, you found a home for one of His creatures."

"Yeah. I—" Gareth paused and cleared his throat. "I want to say thank you. I didn't want to come talk to you about this—either time, really. But I appreciate the fact that you've made time in your schedule for me, for us. I don't know where July and I would be if we hadn't met with you last fall or if I hadn't come back. I might not be finished needing your advice, but for now, you've helped get things back on track. We don't have a perfect marriage..."

"No such thing."

Gareth frowned. "Really? You don't think the majority of couples who have kids have gotten all the kinks worked out of their relationship first?"

Paul's head fell back as he let out a loud guffaw. "Oh my, no. If you had to wait for your marriage to be perfect—your relationship to be ideal—before you had kids, well, no one would have children. You can't wait for perfection before you start a family, just like you can't expect a baby to fix a marriage. Babies just are. They add so many wonderful things to a relationship, but they add strains, too. Even if you did have a mythical perfect marriage when you brought a baby into it, by the time you got home from the hospital that perfection would be soiled like your little one's diaper."

"Huh. I guess I thought that maybe that's one reason... I mean I knew better in my head. But..."

"You wanted it to make sense." Paul nodded. "I understand that. I think we all do that, try to put God into our logical boxes. If something bad happens, or we're denied a blessing, there has to be a reason for it. But sometimes the only reason we know this side of heaven is that He allowed it that He might be glorified. In some way, everything you've gone through will be used to His glory if you'll allow it. That doesn't mean you won't hurt or that you'll ever understand it, but He will use it."

Gareth sighed. "Need to work on that."

"We all do. It's not something that you only learn once and

then handle perfectly from then on. At least in my own life I find that every new trial, every new chance to suffer, brings me right back to my knees where I have to surrender my will and my perception of what's fair and right."

GARETH PROPPED his feet on the deck rail as Millie zoomed around the back yard in the gathering dusk. Had he given up on his own idea of fair and right, like the pastor had said? He was working on it. That had to count for something.

"Hey." July plopped into the chair next to his. "She can really go, can't she?"

He nodded and reached for her hand. "Imagine when she's not just as likely to trip over her own feet as not."

July laughed.

"You're home early. Did you bring work with you?"

She shook her head. "Would you believe I'm down to my last three returns? I should be able to finish them up easily tomorrow. And I'll still be a day ahead of the game. I'll look through and see if there are any of Geoff's clients that I can squeeze in under the wire on Wednesday, but I'm not going to kill myself trying. I've already got the extensions filed and even if they did manage to squeak through the corporate review, I want to double-check for fraud myself. If my name's going on them from here on out, I want everything above board."

That's my girl. He covered her fingers with his. "Have I told you how proud you make me?"

Pink tinged her cheeks. "Not for a while."

He pursed his lips. Had he gotten so wrapped up in his own disappointments that he'd stopped really seeing his wife? "I'm sorry. I've been... struggling. I let myself get caught up in it."

"Seems fair." She flashed a grin. "I did the same in the fall."

They watched Millie in silence as the sun sank behind the trees.

"Did I tell you Lydia's expecting?"

Gareth shook his head. "No. That's good news, right?"

"Yeah. Yeah, it is. I think she was worried I'd be upset. I guess June has known for a while but Lydia wanted to tell me herself." July sighed. "It's hard. No one tells you how difficult it can be to work at having a family—how you're just as likely to damage the family you already have while you're trying to expand it. Why is that, do you think?"

"Maybe the only ones who know are the people who've gone through it... and I know I'm not looking for chances to talk about it. If I could just put it behind me and never think about it again, I probably would. Wouldn't you?"

"Hmm. Probably. Still... I'm grateful that we found our way through it. Even if we're not completely out of the woods, we've found the trail and we're both on it, together. I don't want to be anywhere else." She paused and cleared her throat. "Lydia mentioned a pregnancy loss support group they refer people to at the Center. I... I might think about going sometime."

"I love you." He met her gaze, warmth washing over him. Maybe his love wasn't the same shape and size it was when they said their vows...but who'd want it to be? That had been shiny and largely untested. Now their love was dinged up and some of the edges had lost their shine, but all the rubbing had revealed the strength underneath. He wouldn't trade it.

"I love you, too. Wanna go in and make some popcorn?" July jerked her head toward the door.

Gareth stood and whistled for Millie. "Let's."

31

June paced the length of the kitchen. Naomi screamed in her ear. No amount of walking, bouncing, rocking, singing, or praying seemed to make a difference. Could babies pick up on their parent's anxiety? She glanced at the phone. Why hadn't Faith called? Betty should have signed the papers yesterday. That was the tenth day.

She grabbed the phone and turned it on as she'd done throughout the day today. The dial tone buzzed. She clicked it off. The phone worked. Still. What was going on?

"Shhh. Oh baby, please stop crying." Tears pricked June's eyes. How much was she supposed to be able to handle?

The garage door opened and Toby stomped in, dragging his feet across the welcome mat. "Any news?"

June shook her head.

He frowned and kicked off his shoes and nodded at the baby. "Has she been at this all day again?"

"Yeah. We had a few breaks, but not many. I called the pediatrician. They'll see her tomorrow, but the advice nurse was pretty certain it's just colic. And I'm going to have to work very hard not to punch the next person who says 'just colic' to me."

"Here." Toby reached for Naomi. Her cries stopped as he lifted her off June's shoulder and she let out a huge belch.

June covered her face with her hands. "Oh please... please tell me it hasn't been just gas. I burped her. I even put that gas stuff in her bottles. I've been doing everything..."

She sank to the floor, sobs wracking her shoulders. She couldn't do it. She was the worst parent on the planet.

"Hey. Shh." Toby knelt in front of her and lifted her chin with a finger. "It's nothing you're doing or not doing. You're a wonderful mother. This is hard, for both of us. Heck, all three of us. It's going to get better."

She sniffled and wiped her nose on her sleeve. "Promise?"

He nodded.

She tilted her head to the side. He couldn't know, not for sure. What if she never got any better at this? What if Naomi hated her and only loved him? Or if Betty changed her mind and took the baby back after all? *Would that really be so bad?* She stomped on the thought. It would be that bad—worse than that bad. The sucking hole in her gut stretched wider, leaving more emptiness and nausea in its wake. "Faith still hasn't called."

Toby blew out a breath. Naomi cooed. He chuckled and made a silly face. "Let's call her."

June stood and splashed cold water on her face at the sink. Dabbing with the kitchen towel, she nodded. She'd talked herself out of doing that all day. At this point, it didn't matter if they became a bother... they needed to know. "All right."

Toby took the phone and stood by the refrigerator, dialing the number on the business card stuck there. He hit the speaker button and the ringing filled the space.

"This is Faith."

"Hi Faith, it's Toby and June."

"Hi guys."

June glanced at Toby. She sounded off—certainly not the

cheerful greeting they were used to getting. "We were wondering what was going on..."

"I've been putting off calling you. I keep hoping Betty will show up. We had an appointment yesterday morning. She missed it. I was finally able to get a hold of her and she explained that her car's battery was dead. So we rescheduled for today but she's still a no-show and her phone is going straight to voice mail."

June's breath caught in her throat as her stomach sank. "What... what does that mean?"

"I'm not sure. At this point, I need to get a hold of her to be able to answer that question reliably. I know this is hard, but just hang in there. I'm sure there's a reasonable explanation."

"Are you?"

Toby frowned at her. June shrugged. It was a valid question and she was past the point where she could hold them back.

"I really am. I've had several conversations with Betty over the last ten days. She's very committed to placing. Her family supports her decision, from a distance. There are issues there— between her and her family—but none that should impact the placement. The last message I left, I made sure she has my personal cell and home number. I really think she'll get in touch with me tonight and we'll be back on track tomorrow."

"Okay. Thanks for the update. If you do hear from her tonight, would you let us know? Please?" Toby bounced as Naomi began to fret.

"You're sure? It might be late..."

"We're sure." June leaned over the phone. "We're not getting a ton of sleep anyway."

Faith laughed. "Ah, how I remember those days. All right. I'll be in touch. But if you don't hear from me tonight, try not to worry. I'll for sure touch base with you tomorrow."

"Okay. Thanks, Faith." Toby disconnected the call and bit his lip. "Let's pray."

June nodded. It was the right response...but what words was she supposed to use? Would God leave Naomi with them or had she proven she wasn't able to handle it? She bowed her head as Toby began to pray. A tear slipped down her cheek. *Please, God... don't take her away. I can handle being a parent... I know I can. I just need time.*

32

"I'm so glad you could get away. I didn't think you'd really be free for lunch on the actual last day to get taxes turned in." June sat and angled the stroller so Naomi wasn't in the sun. She turned so she was facing her sister. The courtyard fountain burbled, a subtle, cheery undertone to the early lunchtime noises.

"Would you believe I'm done?" July grinned and tipped her face toward the sun. "I'm going to try and get one more turned in this afternoon. I already filed an extension for them, but since I have the time, I think I can push it through. Either way, I'm going home at five. What brings you out this way?"

"I had to get out of the house before we both went crazy. Faith is supposed to call—well, she was supposed to call last night but she didn't—and let us know what's going on with the paperwork. Betty—the birthmother—didn't show on Monday or yesterday." June clenched her hands into fists in her lap. "I don't know what's going on... it's driving me nuts."

July frowned. "Is that normal?"

"How am I supposed to know?" June threw her hands in the

air. "Faith is all, 'it's going to be fine, just hang in there' but I'm sleep-deprived and losing my mind."

"Shh." July's gaze darted around and she winced. "I'm sorry it's so hard. The sleeping hasn't gotten any better?"

June shook her head. "We went to the pediatrician this morning. They gave me a few suggestions to see if maybe she has some reflux... something has to give though. I can't... I can't keep this up."

July's eyebrows lifted.

June's shoulders drooped. Should she not have said anything? Couldn't her sister try, just for a minute, to understand and sympathize? "It's not that I'm not grateful..."

"No. Stop." July touched June's knee. "I'm sorry. I get that it's been tough. I don't imagine the uncertainty has helped anything, either. I can't say I understand, not fully, but I do know what it's like when you get something you've dreamed about, only to discover that it's not exactly what you thought it'd be. Still wonderful, but not a perfect match to your expectations.'

That was it, exactly. June nodded. "Thanks."

"I can't say it's not hard for me still. But... I want to do better. I'm trying."

"That's all I can ask."

JUNE GAVE a push and set the porch swing rocking. Naomi nestled in her arms, her eyes roaming around. How much could she see? Hadn't she read that babies couldn't focus much beyond a foot at this age? Why did it look like Naomi was watching the clouds? June leaned in and smiled. Naomi's gaze locked with hers and her heart swelled. Sweet girl. She was worth every minute of the sleepless nights.

The phone rang and June snatched it up. "Hello?"

"June, it's Faith. I'm sorry I didn't call last night."

Or for the majority of today... are you sorry for that, too? "It's fine. Did you get a hold of her?"

"Finally, yes. She was in an accident yesterday on her way here."

"Oh. Oh, no. Is she okay?" June's heart took off in a gallop.

"She is now. Last night they were worried; one of her lungs collapsed. At this point, she's stable and they're expecting her to make a full recovery. It'll take some time, obviously."

"Can she still sign the papers?" June hunched her shoulders. That shouldn't be the most important question... but it was. If she was a horrible person because of it, well... so be it.

Faith chuckled. "I'm on my way to the hospital with them now. I went ahead and called one of our attorneys to meet me there. Normally we don't need legal counsel for this, but I want to have, I guess you could call it backup, just on the incredibly remote chance that, down the line, someone questioned her mental state because of the accident."

June bit her lip. That made sense. "Should we wait? I don't want to... I want Naomi to be ours, unquestionably. But if we need to wait for her to be well, we can. We will."

"I'll let her know that's an option, but honestly I think she's as anxious as you and Toby to have this part behind her. It's closure, of sorts, for her. It helps her—and you—move on with the next phase."

"Okay." The tightness in her chest loosened. "Okay. You'll call when it's done?"

"I will. Just a while longer and the hardest part will be behind you."

June hung up and set the phone next to her on the swing. She tapped Naomi's nose with her own. "Hear that, baby girl? It'll be official soon. You'll be mine and I'll be yours. I should call Daddy."

She punched in Toby's cell number and waited. The song

they'd both loved in college played in the distance, growing louder as it continued and the phone rang in her ear.

"Boo." Toby poked his head out and wiggled his phone. "I'm home."

Grinning, June hung up and stood. "Faith's on the way to the hospital with the paperwork for Betty. She—Betty—was in an accident. That's why she missed the appointment."

"But she's okay?"

June nodded and walked into Toby's outstretched arms. She dropped her head on his shoulder. "We're almost officially a family."

33

June looked out over July and Gareth's backyard. Millie dashed around from tree to tree, yipping and chasing after the balls Gareth lobbed for her. Did she ever run out of energy? July sighed and dropped into the chair next to hers.

"Gimme."

June wrinkled her forehead.

July waggled her fingers toward Naomi. "Let me see that niece of mine."

"Really?" June's heart soared as she transferred the baby to her sister's arms.

"Hi there, Naomi. I'm your auntie. I'm the one you come to when your mom says no, got it?" July winked at June and rubbed noses with Naomi. Naomi let out a delighted squeal.

June chuckled. "You're a natural."

"Now that's a sight for sore eyes." Gareth climbed the steps to the deck two at a time and dropped a kiss on July's head. "It's nice, isn't it?"

July nodded. "Go tend the grill. You've had more than your share already. I get to catch up."

June stood, stretching the kinks out of her back. "Where's Toby?"

"He's finishing up the potato salad. Or that's what he said he was going to do... half an hour ago."

"Maybe I should go check..."

Toby slid the door open and stepped through with a huge bowl balanced on plates. Silverware jangled against the sides of the glass he'd tucked it in and a bottle was wedged under his arm. "Steaks ready?"

"Just about. We were getting ready to call in the Marines." Gareth poked the meat, nodded, and turned the dials on the grill. "We're set."

"Perfect timing." Toby's eyes danced. "This was a good idea. A barbecue to celebrate all the paperwork being signed for Naomi, as well as for Millie. Of course we still have post-placement visits to contend with, but you two are free and clear."

"Didn't you say the post-placement visits were basically a formality, nothing more?" Gareth transferred steaks to a platter.

"Basically, yeah. But we still have a few months before everything's one-hundred-percent official. Millie is already there." The bowls and plates in Toby's arms bobbled as he tried to set them down.

June jumped up and helped him unload onto the table. Millie wove around their feet, nipping at their shoelaces.

"Hey. Back up, girlie, or there'll be no table scraps for you." Toby shook his finger at the pup with a grin.

"There will be no table scraps for her anyway." Gareth carried the platter of steaks to the table. "It's not good for her and I don't want her thinking it's okay to beg at the table. Maybe, just maybe, I'll save a little for her bowl later, but nothing from the table. Got it?"

June scooped up the wiggling puppy, giggling when Millie's tongue swiped across her face. "I'm your auntie... you just come sit over by my place whenever your Mom and Dad get strict like that."

"Hey!" July snickered. "That only works with people. Spoiled dogs aren't part of the deal."

June set Millie back down. "Says who?"

"Like that dog's not going to be the most spoiled creature on the planet. I bet she already has four different beds to choose from."

July and Gareth exchanged looks, guilt plainly written on their features.

"Only three. It's not unreasonable for her to be comfortable." Gareth pulled out a chair at the table and sat.

"You keep telling yourself that." Toby held out a chair for June, then sat in the one beside her. He unscrewed the top of the bottle and poured the fizzing apple juice into the cups before passing them around. "Anyway, it's not as if you'll be able to keep her from getting table scraps when you're out of the country. When do you leave?"

July grinned. "Middle of July. Mom and Dad are going to come and house sit for us. That way Millie has someone to love on her and we don't have to worry about finding a good boarding kennel just yet. And they're already planning to try and convince you that Naomi will be old enough for them to watch her overnight."

June shook her head. "Overnight? No chance. But I see some dates in our future. You're sure you're okay with them hanging here while you're out of town?"

"Absolutely."

"Well, I appreciate it. I'm excited that they'll get to come back so soon and spend more time with Naomi, but I wasn't looking forward to figuring out where they could sleep."

"Not to mention they'll go somewhere else. And Millie's enough responsibility that they can't stay at your house for the entire day without interruption." Gareth chuckled. "You can thank us later."

Toby laughed. "I'll thank you now. You're going to take lots of pictures, right? I don't know when we'll manage a trip to the UK at this point. Maybe when Naomi's in high school."

"More pictures than I imagine anyone will want to look at." July reached for Gareth's hand. "I'm still struggling to believe that we're spending an entire month in England, Scotland, and Wales."

June watched as everyone loaded their plates. This was right—exactly right. Maybe everyone didn't have exactly what they wanted, but right didn't mean perfect. And things could still change—still *would* change. The last two years had proved that.

Millie zoomed in circles around the table, trying to put her paws on Gareth's lap. He shooed her down with a gentle ear ruffle. July held Naomi, who looked like she'd drifted off for the time being.

Toby dropped half a steak onto her plate. "You all right?"

She nodded.

"Let's bless the food, I'm starved." Gareth grinned and bowed his head. "Heavenly Father, thank you for bringing us together. Not just for this dinner tonight, but from the very start of our journey as family. You knew, as only You could, that the four of us would encourage, challenge, and sharpen one another. Thank You for the good times we've had, and will continue to have, together. And for the hard times, the ones that stretch us in uncomfortable directions but teach us what You mean by the word 'love.' Amen."

A chorus of 'Amen' fluttered around the table.

Reaching for her glass, June cleared her throat. "Before we dig in, I'd like to propose a toast. To family. It's not always easy or the way you thought it'd be, but when it comes down to it, I wouldn't want it any other way."

They clinked their glasses, laughing. June met July's gaze across the table and smiled. Her sister smiled back over Naomi's head. They'd been stretched and uncomfortable, Gareth had that right.

But the end result, this clearer definition of love, was better than they could have imagined. And it was beautiful.

WANT A FREE BOOK?

If you enjoyed *Love Defined* and would like to read another book of mine, you can receive a free e-book simply by signing up for my newsletter here: http://bit.ly/2goAGvf

SNEAK PEEK OF WISDOM TO KNOW, GRANT US GRACE BOOK 1

Wisdom to Know

Grant Us Grace, book 1

"You look like a prostitute."

Lydia frowned. "Brad likes my legs."

Kevin admired the long, shapely legs of his best friend from where he was sprawled on her living room couch. "Won't you be cold if you show so much of them?"

"It's September, not the middle of January. It's still warm out." Aggravation written across her face, she patted her hem. "Besides, the skirt reaches the end of my fingertips."

"Your elbows are bent."

"That rule shouldn't apply to me, I have long fingers."

Kevin cocked a brow. "You wouldn't wear that to church."

"We're not going to church." Lydia shot him an impish grin. "Besides, there are a couple of guys there who wouldn't usually give me the time of day...maybe if I wore this, I'd get their attention."

"More than likely." Kevin shook his head. "Where are you going? You never did say."

"Dinner downtown, then to a club, in Georgetown I think."

"Bridge club?" He asked hopefully.

Lydia snickered. "Dance. But then you knew that. And before you ask, no, I don't know which club. But," she lifted a red-tipped finger to forestall his comment, "since it's Brad, it'll be either swing or salsa."

Kevin frowned. "Everyone is going to see your underwear in that skirt."

Lydia rolled her eyes.

Kevin started to speak several times before rubbing his forehead. "I'm just trying to look out for you, kiddo."

"Thanks, Mom."

"Didn't you just finish complaining that Brad treats you like an object?"

She gave a grudging nod.

"You think it might have something to do with clothing choices?"

Lydia crossed her arms. "I should be able to wear anything I want and still be treated with respect."

"Sure, in a perfect world. But seriously, Lyd, that outfit..." He paused and considered the short skirt too-snug top and shook his head. "It doesn't scream 'Respect me'."

Pouting, she pushed his feet out of the way and flopped onto the couch beside him. "I appreciate your concern."

Kevin snorted.

"No, I really do." She smiled and patted his knee. "You're like the brother I never had."

He winced.

"Still, a date with your almost fiancé is surely a reason to dress up, right? Or did you want me to wear something like that?" Lydia gestured to a conservative black jacket draped on the arm of the sofa.

"What's wrong with it?"

"That's for work. This is a date. You don't wear work clothes on a date."

Kevin stood, glancing at his watch, "Whatever, Lydia. I drove into McLean to see if you were free tonight, not to be a stand-in for a girlfriend. Or a brother. You look great and you know it." A brief, wistful look flashed across his features. "I'm sure Brad will agree." His hand on the knob of her apartment door, he turned and added with a resigned sigh, "You know where to find me when you get home and need to complain about how he spent the evening undressing you with his eyes."

"That's not fair, Kevin."

"Tell me about it," he muttered, slamming the apartment door behind him.

AUTHOR'S NOTE

Dear Reader,

Writing about June and July has, in many ways, been a challenge for me. The process of exploring their pain brought back memories of my own struggles with infertility and, while June and July aren't specifically modeled after my own journey (or that of anyone I know), there are certainly similarities that nearly any woman who has traveled these paths will understand.

Because I believe fiction should have a taste of reality to it, not everyone in the book gets a fairy tale conclusion to their story. This is, to a large degree, because not everyone who experiences infertility finds complete contentment with their situation, nor does everyone end up with the baby they yearn for. I do believe that with prayer and, perhaps, counseling, everyone can get to a place where they are able to rest in the understanding that God will, somehow, use this for His glory. And I do believe that the girls (and their husbands) have found at least the start of this understanding by the end of the series.

As always, I'd be remiss if I didn't note the incredible people in my life who make writing books a reality for me instead of a dream. Thanks, as ever, to my editor, Lynellen Perry, who takes the lumpy drafts I send her and helps to shape them into what you see today. Any issues or mistakes that remain within these pages are entirely my own. Thanks, also, to my husband who continues to support me in these efforts by watching the kids and telling me (some days more times than should be necessary) that I *can* do this. Love you, honey. And to those who serve as critique partners and beta readers, my undying gratitude for helping me catch where I accidentally swapped wives in the middle of a conversation. I'm definitely not trying to write that kind of novel.

And last, but definitely not least, my thanks to the Heavenly Father—my one desire is that whatever I write would glorify Him and be something He can use in the lives of others.

Thank you for spending time in the pages of my books. Without readers, authors are pointless.

~Elizabeth

DISCUSSION QUESTIONS

1. Were you satisfied with the ending of this series? Why or why not?

2. Have you ever been tempted to over-share with online friends? Has that impacted your real-life relationships at all?

3. Lydia says that adoption is something easy to support in theory but sometimes harder when it's something you're facing personally. Do you agree or disagree?

4. If you've never experienced infertility, has this series helped you understand those who have experienced it better? How?

5. If you have struggled with infertility, in what ways was your journey similar and different from that of June and July?

6. Does Betty's revelation about her own struggles with fertility help you understand her treatment of the girls at all?

7. We don't see July wrestle with her grief very much. Do you think she's simply in deep denial or has she

just accepted it and made a conscious decision to move on?

8. June experiences mild post-partum depression. Was it surprising to you to discover that this can plague adoptive parents? Why or why not?

9. Do you believe adoptive parents are allowed to struggle with how hard it is to be a new parent or should they just suck it up since it's something they fought so hard to achieve?

10. Over the course of this series, the relationships between the sisters, as well as the relationships within the couples, have been redefined. Have you ever been in a situation where hardship has had this effect on your relationships? What was the most helpful thing during that time?

11. Pastor Brown says that perfect marriages aren't required before a couple has a child. Do you agree or disagree? Why?

RESOURCES

National Council for Adoption
www.adoptioncouncil.org

American Academy of Adoption Attorneys
www.adoptionattorneys.org

National Infertility Association
www.resolve.org

Support for grieving miscarriage, stillbirth, or child death
www.silentgrief.com

ABOUT THE AUTHOR

Elizabeth Maddrey is a semi-reformed computer geek and homeschooling mother of two who lives in the suburbs of Washington D.C. When she isn't writing, Elizabeth is a voracious consumer of books. She loves to write about Christians who struggle through their lives, dealing with sin and receiving God's grace on their way to their own romantic happily ever after.

Visit her website at www.ElizabethMaddrey.com

www.ingramcontent.com/pod-product-compliance
Lightning Source LLC
Chambersburg PA
CBHW060929180626
46817CB00004B/1455